JIMMY ZEST

Sam McBratney grew up in County Antrim, Northern Ireland, and still lives and works there. Once a teacher, he has now been a writer for over thirty years. He has written books for children of all ages and his work is known all over the world. His international awards include the Abby (America), the Silveren Griffel (Holland) and the Bisto (Ireland). His picture book *Guess How Much I Love You* is one of the most successful books in the history of children's literature.

Sam and his wife live surrounded by their children and grandchildren, and their tortoise, Mabel – who is the size of a dinner-plate.

Also by Sam McBratney

Zesty

JIMMY ZEST

Sam McBratney

Illustrated by Tim Archbold

MACMILLAN CHILDREN'S BOOKS

First published 1982 by Hamish Hamilton Children's Books
This edition published in 2002 by Macmillan Children's Books
a division of Macmillan Publishers Limited
20 New Wharf Road, London N1 9RR
Basingstoke and Oxford
www.panmacmillan.com

Associated companies throughout the world

ISBN 0 330 40067 3

1 3 5 7 9 8 6 4 2

A CIP catalogue record for this book is available from the British Library.

Typeset by SX Composing DTP, Rayleigh, Essex
Printed and bound in Great Britain by Mackays of Chatham plc, Kent

Contents

– 1 –

Jimmy Zest's
Egg Box Wonder

Once Jimmy Zest started collecting egg boxes it became a habit.

This is the sort of thing that he did. When his mum came back from the shops he met her at the door to help her carry in the parcels. In the kitchen his mum stood on a stool and Jimmy Zest reached her stuff out of the parcels to put it into the cupboards – sugar, baked beans, biscuits – all that sort of thing.

"Huh," said Jimmy Zest, "didn't you get any eggs?"

His mum looked down at him from a great height.

"I got eggs yesterday," she said, not a bit pleased. "Do you want this family eating eggs until we've all turned into chickens? Eggs, eggs, eggs."

Jimmy Zest did not want eggs, eggs, eggs. He wanted boxes, boxes, boxes.

One day – it was a Saturday – he got his mum into big trouble in the supermarket.

1

The supermarket was a huge place, the kind of place some children got lost in. But Jimmy Zest knew how to look after himself. And he knew where they kept their eggs.

The egg shelf was always packed full with beautiful boxes. They had grey boxes, pink boxes, cardboard egg boxes, plastic egg boxes. There was only one thing wrong with them. They had eggs in them.

On this particular Saturday, Jimmy Zest didn't let that stop him. While his mum was at the cheese counter, he filled a plastic bag with egg boxes.

Nobody saw him – or so he thought. When they got to the checkout the woman at the till pointed to his plastic bag and said to his mum, "Is there anything in that bag? What has he got in that bag?"

Jimmy Zest slid the bag round the back of his legs to hide it.

"Oh, it's just meat," his mum said nicely. "It's already paid for."

By this time there was a man standing beside them. Jimmy Zest did not like the look of him. He was bald and fierce.

"I'm afraid there's more than meat in *that* bag, madam," he said, as he scratched his head with one finger.

2

So there was, of course. One look at the face of
Jimmy Zest told all. There might just as well have
been a sign round his neck saying: THIEF.

"What have you got in that bag?" his mum
snapped at him.

The bald man bent down and opened it.

"It's full of eggs," he declared.

"It's not," said Jimmy Zest.

"Oh but it *is*," the man said, showing an angry
mouthful of twisted teeth.

Jimmy Zest led them all the way back to the

egg shelf, where he stopped and pointed at three dozen brown eggs, all out of their boxes.

"Those are eggs without boxes," said Jimmy Zest. "In here, in my bag, I've got boxes without eggs."

His mum stood with her mouth open, waiting for words to happen.

"Oh! You little . . . wart! Oh!" She turned to the bald man. "*You* talk to him. Tell him you'll put him in jail."

The man was scratching his head again, just where the hair started.

"Well, I don't think we could put him in jail, exactly. If he'd taken the eggs and left the boxes – that might have been different."

"I don't want eggs," said Jimmy Zest. "Only boxes."

They left the man still scratching his head. Jimmy Zest thought that maybe, if he stopped scratching, his hair wouldn't get loose and fall out.

Back home, his mum looked as if she meant business. Slap! Bang! Wallop! she went round his legs. Then she sent him up to his room.

The limping Jimmy Zest went up the stairs as if he had just been in a fight with a hairy, great monster.

He set his collection of egg boxes out on his

bed. He had forty-eight of the wonderful things, which wasn't bad going.

He had only been collecting for a week.

Monday was the next school day. Jimmy Zest could hardly wait for it. On Monday morning he sneaked out with his schoolbag on his back and a plastic bag in his hand.

There was a jigsaw in the bag. And a Teddy. And a Slinky toy that could walk down the stairs.

At break-time the teacher left the room with a flask full of coffee under her arm. Jimmy Zest asked his friend Legweak to stand guard at the door. Then he set out his toys on the teacher's table and stood behind it.

"Roll up, roll up," he shouted.

He felt like a man at the market with one small stall.

"I'm selling these toys," he said to his friends.

Penny Brown was there; Mandy Taylor, too. And Knuckles and Shorty, the twins. A boy called Philip McGowan jumped eagerly down from the radiator as Jimmy Zest held up a box and gave it a rattle.

"This jigsaw has all its pieces but two. I'm selling it for two egg boxes."

Nobody seemed very interested. Knuckles said,

"What use is a jigsaw with two bits lost?"

"What use are two egg boxes?" said Jimmy Zest, quick as a flash. He saw some heads nodding at that, so he picked up the Slinky.

"This Slinky – ten egg boxes."

"Ten!" declared Philip McGowan, otherwise known as Gowso.

"You want it for nothing?" Jimmy Zest snapped at Gowso. "It can walk down the stairs on its own, you know."

Mandy Taylor said, "Oh, I'd love a Slinky."

Now they were interested. He had them now.

6

"This Teddy – three egg boxes."

This caused a fuss.

"It's only got one leg."

"Come on now, Zesty."

"Where's its other eye?"

"Was it your great-granny's?"

"How'd you like somebody to chew *your* ears off, Zesty?"

There was so much criticism of the Teddy that Jimmy Zest lowered its price.

"OK. Seeing that it's not perfect – one egg box."

Penny Brown put her name down for the Teddy because, she said, she felt sorry for the poor little thing.

Word came from Legweak that the teacher was coming back. Jimmy Zest warned them to bring in the egg boxes tomorrow or they would get no toys.

On Wednesday night he set his collection out on the bed to count it.

There was not enough room for all the boxes on the bed.

Later that week Jimmy Zest took a walk round the shops where he lived. The first shop was a butcher's. There was a sign on the door:

DOGS ENTER THIS SHOP
AT THEIR OWN RISK.

The sign was low down on the door, as if the butcher expected dogs to read it.

Jimmy Zest went in.

"Have you any egg boxes, Mr Buckley?"

Mr Buckley was standing behind a table with a thick, wooden top. Mr Buckley was cutting a lump of meat with a big knife.

He stopped to glare at Jimmy Zest.

"Have I any *what*?"

"Egg boxes."

Mr Buckley held up his knife. "What's that?"

"A big sharp knife."

"That's a butcher's knife," he roared. "I'm a *butcher*. I cut up pigs and cows."

Jimmy Zest turned away from the big red face above him. He pointed at a row of plucked chickens. "When I saw the chickens, I thought you might have eggs. And boxes, too, of course."

"Have you not heard?" Mr Buckley said very nastily. "They don't lay eggs when they're dead. By the time they get to me, boy, their egg-laying days are well and truly over. Goodbye."

Jimmy Zest did not bother to try the vegetable shop, but the grocer's was just round the corner. The grocer had a sign in his window, too, but it was not meant for clever dogs to read. It was meant for Jimmy Zest and people like him.

It said:

SORRY – NO EGG BOXES.

PLEASE DON'T ASK.

Jimmy Zest was not stupid. He knew what was happening. People like Knuckles and Shorty and Penny Brown and Gowso had been here before him, trying to get egg boxes to bring into school to buy his toys. They were all at it, the copy-cats.

Egg boxes were getting scarce.

It was Friday, and Knuckles and Shorty were on their way to school. It was not their favourite place, so they were not in much of a hurry.

Shorty was carrying a bag full of egg boxes. Knuckles had his hands in his pockets. He never carried anything. He was ten minutes older than Shorty and pushed his brother around a bit.

They were talking about Jimmy Zest. "*Why* does he want them?" Knuckles was saying. "Why, why, why?"

"I'm not worried why he wants them," Shorty said. "I got a toy crane off him yesterday. I just hope he keeps on wanting them, that's all."

But Knuckles had a worried look on his face. He didn't trust Jimmy Zest. Maybe there was money to be made out of egg boxes – or something.

Jimmy Zest's mum was cleaning out his room on Saturday morning. She was in a good mood, and very pleased with Jimmy.

"Not a toy in sight," she said to herself, "everything neat and tidy. Perhaps he's changed."

Even his silly egg boxes were neatly stacked away.

Then she began to wonder. His room usually looked as if the contents of a giant pocket had been emptied all over the floor.

Where *were* his toys?

They were not in the drawers. They were not in the wardrobe. Under his bed she found only egg boxes. It was all very peculiar, for it seemed that the only toys her son had to his name were a dartboard, an etch-a-sketch and a space-hopper out in the garage.

The phone rang. "Hello," she heard, "is that the mother of Jimmy Zest?"

She just *knew* it was trouble. She wished she

could say, "Sorry, wrong number," and put the phone down. But she had to admit it. "Yes, I'm his mother."

"I'm not complaining," the voice said. "I'm really not complaining at all, Mrs Zest, but . . . I thought you should know."

"What? What should I know?"

"Well, he's going round the houses asking people for egg boxes. And, you know, he's got a wheelbarrow with him."

As soon as he came through the door, Jimmy Zest knew that he was in bother. It always meant trouble when they stood together like that, side by side, his mum and dad.

His mum spoke first. "Where are your toys?"

"Not anywhere special."

"Where's that?"

"Not all in one place."

"*Where* are they?"

He had to tell. Sold. For egg boxes. To the boys in school. And a girl or two as well.

"Oh, my heavens," his mum said. "He hasn't a toy left in the house."

Then an awful look came over her face. "Where's Teddy?"

"Sold."

His mum turned and buried her face in his

dad's shoulder. "Oh no, he's gone and sold my Teddy. I've had him since I was a baby and they don't even *make* them like that any more."

His dad patted his mum on the back to comfort her. He looked a bit embarrassed by the whole thing, and a little curious, too.

"How much did you get for Teddy?" he asked.

"One egg box. It wasn't in very good condition, you know," said Jimmy Zest. His mum was going on as if the thing was brand new.

They ganged up on him then – once his mother had recovered from the shock. Since his parents failed to realize the importance of egg boxes, Jimmy Zest had to shift armful after armful from his bedroom to the garage.

It took him ages.

Knuckles and Shorty had a great weekend. They spent most of their time gathering up stuff for their bonfire, which was coming along very nicely. They had quite a few branches and quite a few rubber tyres. The bonfire was nearly ready.

The twins were experts on bonfires. They liked to have one every six weeks or so – if they could get the stuff to burn. Knuckles often said that if it wasn't for school they could easily have a bonfire every three weeks.

Their great weekend was brought to an end by school on Monday. They had a bad day. It started when the teacher asked them how their project was coming along.

Knuckles had to admit that he hadn't even started. Neither had Shorty.

The teacher was furious. "*Everybody* has started. Penny, what is your project?"

"Graveyards, Miss Quick."

"Jimmy Zest?"

"Dinosaurs, Miss."

"Mandy?"

"Foreign food, Miss Quick."

Miss Quick turned to the twins. "You see? How dare you tell me you haven't started. What are you interested in?"

"Bonfires, Miss."

This answer made the teacher blink. "What do you mean, bonfires? Explain."

Knuckles explained that what he loved to do best in all the world was to build a bonfire. He and Shorty did it all the time in the field beside their house.

"Don't be silly," the teacher said, "you can't light a bonfire when you like. You must have a reason, like Guy Fawkes' day."

"Shorty and me don't need a reason, Miss.

13

When we gather up the stuff, we go ahead and burn it."

"Then the problem is solved," the teacher said. "You two will do your project on bonfires!"

At lunch-time the twins went looking for Jimmy Zest. They paid four egg boxes for a dartboard and seven for an etch-a-sketch.

Penny Brown saw them and came over for a chat.

"There are some things I don't like about Jimmy Zest," she said. "I admire him in some ways, of course, but he definitely has his bad points."

"What like?" Shorty asked her. He was very fond of Penny Brown.

"Well, he's a squirrel, a greedy squirrel of the human kind. He's got every egg box in the neighbourhood in his garage. Every last one. I think it's terrible."

Knuckles began to feel uncomfortable. Penny Brown was a clever girl. Did she think that Zesty was making money out of egg boxes?

"Who cares?" he said bravely. "I've got his etch-a-sketch."

"And I've got his dartboard," added Shorty.

Penny Brown waved a hand, as if to dismiss their foolish argument. "Last year, when we wanted to go hunting wasps, who had all the jam-jars? Huh? Zesty. You know that gorgeous hat he has, with one hundred and fifteen badges on it? You know the one? Where did he get the badges?"

Knuckles and Shorty hung their heads in shame.

"Yes," Penny Brown went on, "off you and me and Legweak. And what did he swap them for? Huh? The insides of toilet rolls. The stiff cardboard bit. He knew we would want them, because that was the week *Blue Peter* showed you how to make a home-made kaleidoscope."

Penny Brown paused. Shorty was already in a rage against Jimmy Zest. Knuckles had his hands out of his pockets, which was a bad sign for somebody.

"How many of us made a kaleidoscope out of our toilet roll insides?" Triumphantly, she waited. Knuckles smashed his fist against the bark of a tree and hurt himself as Penny Brown finished. "Nobody!"

There was a violent silence. If Jimmy Zest had walked into view at that moment, Shorty and Knuckles would have torn him apart.

"I think," said Penny, "that we should ask that greedy squirrel some questions."

They waited for him after school. Penny Brown was very firm with Knuckles and Shorty. "Now no nonsense," she said to them, as if they were her pet gorillas. "I don't want any rough stuff. Jimmy Zest is a civilized person. He's not *all* bad."

The civilized Jimmy Zest came walking out of school, swinging his plastic bag. Penny Brown, Knuckles and Shorty fell into step beside him.

"We think you're a genius, Zesty," said Penny. "Don't we, Knuckles? Don't we, Shorty?"

The twins looked a bit confused. They didn't see how a squirrel could become a genius just like that. Penny went on, "I see you've got something in your plastic bag. I wonder what?"

"Guess," said Jimmy Zest.

"Egg boxes."

"Right."

"Whose were they?"

"Shorty and Knuckles gave me some. And I got some off the craft teacher."

"You *are* a genius, Jimmy Zest," said Penny Brown. There was genuine admiration in her voice.

Then she said, "We think we have rights, you know. We want to know why you want all these egg boxes, don't we, Shorty? Don't we Knuckles? How many have you?"

"Nearly enough."

"Nearly enough to what?"

"Nearly enough to do."

Knuckles had heard enough to do him, too. "Listen," he said, "there's something funny going on. I want my egg boxes back."

Shorty added, "You can have your dartboard back. We've got no darts anyway, Knuckles and me."

"The darts are extra," said Jimmy Zest. "Two egg boxes each."

Tempers were rising. Penny Brown stamped her foot.

"You're nothing but a human squirrel, Jimmy Zest. How can you be so unreasonable? We'll find out your secret, you know."

*

It was nearly half past eight, and very dark. Penny Brown waited at the shops for Knuckles and Shorty.

Eventually they showed up, eating crisps out of one packet. Knuckles had his hand in his pockets and Shorty was feeding him crisps. "What kept you?" Penny raged at them. "I've been waiting for ages. It's not a summer's night, you know."

Shorty crumpled the crisp bag and stuck it in somebody's hedge.

"What's the hurry?" said Knuckles. "The later the better."

Penny Brown tapped her wrist. "Listen. You two might be able to run the streets till all hours, but *I* come from a respectable home. And I have to be in soon. So come on."

They went along the road as far as Jimmy Zest's house. Quietly, they tiptoed up his drive. They could hear his TV blaring as they went by. It was nice and dark round the back of his house.

"Go on!" Penny whispered to the boys. "Do your stuff."

The twins went prowling. Penny waited as they tried to find a way into the garage. She had every confidence in Shorty and Knuckles, for they were always talking about their grandfather who had been a cat burglar until the police caught him.

Penny Brown was not too sure what a cat burglar did, but she knew it had nothing to do with stealing cats.

She felt awfully wicked. It was a terrible thing to break into somebody's garage, but it would be worth it just to see what Jimmy Zest was up to. It was his own fault for being such a squirrel. She couldn't wait to see his face in the morning when he found out that everybody knew his secret.

Anyway, they weren't going to actually *steal* anything, except a look.

The minutes passed. Knuckles and Shorty stood whispering together. Then they admitted it.

They couldn't find a way into the garage – not unless they broke a window.

Penny was not having any broken windows. "You snooks!" she raged quietly. "You told me that your grandfather was a cat burglar."

Knuckles was very offended by the scorn in her voice. "He was."

"Then it doesn't run in the family, does it?"

Suddenly, a light went on. Penny clapped a hand over her mouth. The light dazzled her. Knuckles's hands came out of his pockets so fast that he almost ripped his trousers off. A man came running out and grabbed the twins.

"Got you! After my car, were you? We'll see about that. And you, girl, you stay where you are.

I can be just as rough with girl thieves, make no mistake about that."

The man dragged them into the living room through his back door. The whole house seemed to be coming alive with noise and light.

Penny felt so ashamed. Jimmy Zest was there, in his pyjamas. He had blue pyjamas, with sharks all over them. He actually winked at her!

"Now then," the man said, "let's find out who you are."

Jimmy Zest looked at Penny and smiled. Then he lifted the phone. "Shall I give the police a buzz, Dad?"

Penny started to cry. She couldn't help it. It was the shame of being caught in the company of people who were descended from cat burglars.

Then Shorty spoke. Penny really admired him for it.

"Not at all," Shorty said. "You needn't call the police. It's us, Zesty. It's only old Knuckles and me." Shorty looked up at Mr Zest as if he was his Sunday School teacher. "Don't worry, Mister, Zesty and us are mates."

That settled it. Mr Zest let them go. Penny explained how she was from a respectable home, she wasn't a burglar of any sort. She told Mr Zest that his son, Jimmy, had every egg box in the neighbourhood under lock and key and that all they were trying to do was take a *look* in the garage. They weren't going to *steal* anything.

Penny, Shorty and Knuckles walked down the drive of Jimmy Zest's house together. Penny stopped at the gate. There was something she simply had to say.

"Shorty," she said, "I admit it. I've underestimated you. You were wonderful tonight!"

Shorty, who was a bit slow, hadn't a clue what she was talking about. He said, "Would you like to come to our bonfire? It's the day after tomorrow. You could declare it open."

Now it was Penny's turn to be puzzled. "Declare what open?"

"Our bonfire. We could tie a big ribbon round it and you could cut it with scissors, the way they do with motorways and things."

Penny looked at Knuckles, then at her watch and saw that she must dash home.

Knuckles and Shorty headed down the road to see if they could beg, steal or borrow a hamburger from the chippie.

Ten minutes later, Knuckles and Shorty had a stroke of the most fantastic luck. They were coming back up the road, sharing a hamburger between them, when they saw Jimmy Zest's dad reversing his car out of his garage. The lights of the car lit up every corner inside the garage. In that second, Knuckles and Shorty saw Jimmy Zest's secret in all its glory.

He had built a monster in his garage – out of egg boxes!

The twins were very impressed by Jimmy Zest's monster. It seemed to go all the way up to the roof. It had a big ugly head and a long tail.

Shorty's eyes bulged. "Did you see that! What was that thing? A big dragon?"

Knuckles smiled, a nasty, curling-up-at-one-corner sort of smile.

"That's no big dragon," he said craftily, "that's a ready-made egg box bonfire."

In school the next morning, Jimmy Zest walked up to the teacher with his dinosaur project in his hand.

"I was just wondering, Miss, what we're going to be doing this morning?"

"Maths."

Bad news.

"It's just that I had other plans. Would you mind if I got on with my dinosaur project?"

"I would mind, yes."

"You see, I've got a section to write on how Dimetrodon uses his fin to catch the heat of the sun."

"Dimetrodon will have to wait, then. You'll do what everyone else does, James Zest."

She called the roll, then. Shorty didn't answer to his name, and neither did Knuckles. Jimmy Zest wondered where they were.

Penny Brown spent the morning trying to keep out of Jimmy Zest's way. She still felt very embarrassed about last night. Then, at lunch-time, he suddenly appeared out of nowhere and sat down beside her.

She felt like Little Miss Muffet, when the spider came. What was she going to say to him about trying to break into his garage? All she could think of was how he had sharks all over his blue pyjamas.

"Hello, Penelope," said Jimmy Zest.

The snook. He always called her Penelope, not Penny like everybody else. She wondered what he wanted.

"Penelope, would you give me back Teddy?"

So that was it! He wanted his Teddy.

"You're not getting it. I bought it."

"Well, it's just that my mum cries every night. She misses him, Penelope."

Penny Brown turned right round to look at Jimmy Zest to see if he was lying.

"She doesn't. Does she?"

Jimmy Zest shook his head sadly.

"She worries."

"About a Teddy?"

"She worries about its health. You know how old it is, Penelope."

Penny Brown thought how it was a great pity that people didn't turn blue or something when they told lies. Then at least you would know.

She hardened her heart. "I wouldn't give it back for ten egg boxes."

Jimmy Zest looked a picture of misery. He got up as if his legs had suddenly grown old and weary. "Then write her a note, Penelope, and tell her Teddy's OK. She'll sleep better."

Penny's eyes narrowed to vicious points. "You really are mean, Zesty. Imagine selling your mum's Teddy. That's the meanest thing I ever heard of."

But she got no answer. Jimmy Zest had got

25

tired of listening to her and was running across the playground.

Shorty and Knuckles came into school in the afternoon. The teacher seemed disappointed to see them, for the class had been quiet all morning.

"Where were *you* this morning?" she asked Knuckles.

"I had a headache, Miss."

"How painful. And you?"

"I had a headache too, Miss."

The teacher took a deep breath. "That's fine, then. You have the same colour of hair, the same eyes, the same head, I suppose it's only right and proper that you should have the same headache. Go and sit down, you pair of absolute scoundrels."

Twice during the afternoon, Jimmy Zest caught Shorty and Knuckles looking over at him. Each time, they looked away and giggled.

Jimmy Zest got a funny feeling about those two. He began to fidget. Why did the twins keep looking at him? Where had they been all morning?

When the school bell rang for the end of classes, Jimmy Zest ran up the road and arrived at his garage with his mouth dry and his tongue hanging out to find that his worst fears were true.

His model dinosaur had gone!

The furious Jimmy Zest kicked his space-hopper

26

up and down the garage. "Knuckles and Shorty are going to die," he promised. His space-hopper went booming into the tin door of the garage.

He ran into the house, but his mother was worse than useless. "It couldn't be gone, that big thing. Your father can hardly get his car into the garage for the size of it. Who would *want* it for goodness sake?" Then, "Is it really *gone*?"

It was gone, all right. Jimmy Zest threw his leg over his bike and started pedalling. That dinosaur was the finest thing he'd made in his whole life – his greatest triumph.

"Knuckles and Shorty are going to die!" he yelled out loud as he pedalled like fury down the road.

Then he stopped. He didn't know exactly where Knuckles and Shorty lived.

But he knew where Penelope Brown lived! And she was in it with them. He rode his bike through her gate, right into the middle of the front garden. He threw his bike down and left it with its front wheel

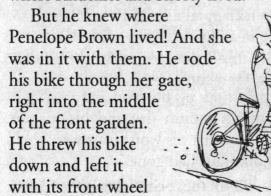

spinning. "Come out, you thief. Come out, come out."

Just to make sure she knew he was there, he gave the bell of his bike a good ring.

Her mum appeared first. She put her head out of an upstairs window and looked down at him with great curiosity. Then Penelope Brown opened the front door.

"I suppose you're here to tell about last night," she said. "Well you needn't bother, you tell-tale tit. My mum's not in. Anyway, she wouldn't listen to you."

Penelope Brown's mother leaned out of the window even further, even more curious.

"And another thing," her daughter went on, "if you tell my mum about last night you'll never get the rotten Teddy back."

Above Penny Brown's head, her mum gave a little cough. "Ahem! What's this about last night?"

Penny Brown clapped a hand to her mouth so hard that she almost knocked her teeth out.

"Penelope! I think that person in the garden should come in for a cup of tea."

"I don't like tea," said that person in the garden, Jimmy Zest.

"Milk, then."

"I don't like milk either."

"Shame on you, all those cows doing their best.

I'm not giving you lemonade to puff out your stomach." Mrs Brown closed the window and came downstairs anyway.

Jimmy Zest told her that her daughter Penny was hanging around at night with known criminals. That made her forget about cows and their lovely milk. He also pointed out that Penelope Brown had helped to steal an eight foot model dinosaur out of his garage that very morning.

"I didn't, I didn't," said Penny. "I was in school, Zesty."

"That doesn't matter," said Jimmy Zest. "It was your plan."

Everybody was quiet, including Penny Brown's mum. She sat looking at Jimmy Zest with a funny expression on her face, as if she had found something absolutely new in life.

"Are you the one who collects egg boxes?"

"I was," said the miserable Jimmy Zest.

With her chin in her hands, Penny Brown sat wondering how she could convince Zesty that she had nothing to do with stealing his dinosaur. She had only wanted a *look* to find out his secret. If only he had told them he was making a model, that would have been enough.

Suddenly, she spoke. "Oh, flute! I know what's happening. I know what they're going to do!"

"What?"

"They're going to burn it. Your dinosaur is in their bonfire. It's going to go up in smoke."

"How do you know?"

"I know. Shorty asked me to declare their bonfire open. I didn't know what to say."

"I never heard of anybody opening a bonfire," her mother said.

"Well that's it then," said Jimmy Zest.

It was always the same. When he was four, he built a monster sandcastle on the beach. Donkeys came along and wrecked it. When he was six he made a paper dart six foot long. It got run over by a lorry in the street. And now, here was his greatest achievement, an eight foot dinosaur, about to go up in smoke. It was enough to make you sick.

Penny got up. "Come on, Zesty, we might be able to save it yet. I know where their bonfire is. I'll get my bike."

The field where Knuckles and Shorty held their bonfires was a remarkable sight. All over it, like gigantic black dots, could be seen the scorched earth where the twins had lit bonfires on other occasions.

"Look," said Penny.

There it was, on top of the pile of planks, branches, paper and rubber tyres – his dinosaur.

They had taken it apart, of course. The tail was near the bottom. Jimmy Zest thought that it could be easily rescued. But the two big legs seemed to be well stuck in. And right at the top of the heap was the splendid head of Tyrannosaurus Rex.

Jimmy Zest felt as if a fire had been lit inside *him*.

"They're going to die," he muttered. "I'm going to rush them, now."

Penny told him not to be silly. She said they would give him black eyes and a bleeding nose.

"Listen, I've got a better idea. I think I know how to get your dinosaur back."

*

The next day, Penny walked home from school with Shorty. They talked about graveyards and dinosaurs. Shorty did some talking about bonfires.

Then Penny said, "I've got some planks in my garage. You could have them for your bonfire if you like. But it would take a strong person to lift them down."

"*I'm* a strong person," said Shorty. He bent his arm and pointed to his bicep. "Feel that."

Penny squeezed his arm with a finger and thumb.

"I think you would do," she said.

In her garage she pointed to a ledge near the roof. Up there her father had stored planks of wood.

"That's where you

have to go, Shorty," she said, "but take off your shoes."

Shorty looked down at his feet. "My shoes? Why?"

"You're a cat burglar, aren't you? Your grandpa would have taken off *his* shoes."

Off came Shorty's shoes and up the ladder he went. He had odd socks on, probably because he and Knuckles weren't fussy about whose they put on in the morning.

Once Shorty was up on the ledge, Jimmy Zest crawled out from his hiding place under a work bench. He and Penny Brown stood looking up at their prisoner.

Slowly, it dawned on Shorty what had happened. He looked from one to the other, then at the ground, then at his socks. "What am I up here for?" he asked.

"You're a prisoner. We're going to exchange you for my egg box dinosaur."

"You mean I'm kidnapped?" Shorty sounded quite proud. Then he said, "I don't want to be kidnapped. I'll jump."

"I doubt it," said Penny.

"If you do, you'll break your legs. Anyway, the door will be locked."

"You wait until Knuckles finds out about this, Zesty," Shorty warned.

They left Shorty up on the ledge and came out of the garage. Jimmy Zest kept an eye on Shorty through the window, just in case he did anything stupid.

Penny had the note already written.

> *Knuckles, we've got Shorty. Give me*
> *back my dinosaur and we'll give you*
> *back Shorty.*
>
> *Jimmy Z.*

An argument started about who was going to take the note. Jimmy Zest wanted to go, but Penny said he was stupid. "Knuckles will start a fight if you go. He'll pull you off your bike."

Jimmy Zest put up his hands. "Let him try. Just let him try."

"Look, Knuckles is far better than you at that sort of thing. He does it every day. He'll probably not hit a girl."

It was agreed. Penny took the note. Jimmy Zest kept watching Shorty, who sat staring moodily at his feet as if it was their fault that he'd been kidnapped.

After about fifteen minutes Penny came back with a dirty mark under her eye. She got off her bike, looking serious.

"That snook Knuckles *does* hit girls. He's not civilized, Zesty."

Jimmy Zest was not in the least surprised. Knuckles was quite capable of hitting anything that moved.

"What did he say about the note?"

Penny shook her head. "He says we can keep Shorty all night for all *he* cares."

Jimmy Zest could hardly believe it. "He said that? About his brother? His *twin* brother?"

Penny nodded in agreement. "Doesn't it just make you despise him? I told him he was a dirty rat and that brothers are supposed to stick together. They even have the same headache, for goodness' sake. Guess what he told me, Zesty."

"I couldn't."

"He told me he'd stick me in his bonfire if I didn't shut my big mouth – that's when I hit him a kick on the shin. And that's when he gave me this."

Penny pointed to a small bruise under her eye and, after a pause for some sympathy from Jimmy Zest, they went into the garage to tell Shorty the news.

Jimmy Zest carried over the ladder and said, "OK, Shorty, you can go."

Down came Shorty with a grin on his face as he reached for his shoes. "Didn't I tell you? I told you Knuckles would sort you two out."

Penny gave him the bad news, that Knuckles didn't care about him one bit, he was only interested in that silly big bonfire of his.

Shorty stood still for a moment with his right shoe in his hand. "*What* did Knuckles say?"

"He said we could keep you all night for all he cares."

"He didn't say that. You're a liar."

Penny wagged a finger at him. "I'm not like you, Shorty Alexander, I don't tell lies."

The brain of Shorty did work, but it worked exceedingly slowly. "You mean they'd rather . . . Knuckles would rather . . . he'd rather keep all those egg boxes than *me?*"

At first, Shorty looked very miserable and very hurt. Then his face clouded over with anger. "Huh," he said.

It occurred to Jimmy Zest that maybe Penny and he were in a spot of bother.

But Shorty wasn't angry at them. "Listen, Zesty," he said, "nobody's going to let me get kidnapped. I'll help you get your big dragon back."

Shorty stayed in Penny Brown's house and had a very nice tea. Then they called for the ready-and-waiting Jimmy Zest and went off to rescue his dinosaur.

Shorty wanted to wait until after dark but, as Jimmy Zest pointed out, they might be too late then. The bonfire might be lit. They were going to have to do the job in broad daylight.

They got down on their knees and sneaked through the long grass until they had almost reached the edge of the bonfire. Shorty stuck up his head to see who was about.

Nobody. The place was deserted.

"Come on," Shorty yelled, "quick. Before he sees us!"

In a fit of excitement, Jimmy Zest ran up the side of the bonfire and sank up to his waist in rubbish.

Shorty made it look easy. He was up the bonfire in no time, and brought the dinosaur head safely to the ground. Penny tried to carry the body away, but some of the egg boxes came loose as she pulled.

"Oh, Zesty, it's coming apart," she shouted.

The struggling Jimmy Zest fought to get out of the hole he was in.

"Never mind the egg boxes," he shouted, "get me out before Knuckles shows up."

It was Shorty who did the real work. While Jimmy Zest and Penny Brown pranced about the bonfire trying to keep their balance, he rescued two dinosaur legs as well as the head.

"Come on," he shouted, "leave that other bit. We'll have to come back for the rest."

When they came back for the rest, however, they got a surprise. Shorty climbed up the bonfire to get the body and, at that moment, Knuckles appeared.

A few seconds passed before he realized what was happening. He stared at his bonfire, now much flatter than it had been, then at Shorty, who was standing with the last bit of dinosaur in his hands.

Furiously, Knuckles pulled his hands out of his pockets. He had a box of matches.

"I'll fix you," he snarled as he put a match to his bonfire.

Shorty began to do a little dance. "Knuckles, it's me, Shorty. Put it out. Put it out."

By now the wind had begun to fan up a very satisfactory flame which ran up the side of the bonfire with an ominous crackling noise. Jimmy Zest shouted, "Drop the dinosaur, Shorty. Save yourself."

Even Knuckles seemed alarmed at what he had done, and shouted, "Jump will you – jump!"

They needn't have worried. Perhaps it had something to do with the smoke going up his nose, but Shorty's brain worked like lightning. He threw the bit of dinosaur high into the air and came flying down the side of the bonfire so fast that his feet hardly seemed to touch it. He didn't even stop when he got to the bottom. He kept right on going, straight into his brother, flinging out wild punches and yelling like a mad thing, "Burn me up, would you," – wallop – "you'll not burn me up in a hurry," – wallop – "I'll ruin you," – wallop – "some brother!"

Knuckles, of course, defended himself, and did some walloping of his own. Jimmy Zest and Penny Brown picked up the last bit of dinosaur and made off with it at top speed.

After a while they stopped and looked back. The bonfire was still blazing away. And beside it, on the ground, Knuckles and Shorty were still at it hammer and tongs.

The following night Mrs Zest heard a knock at her front door. She thought it must be the milkman looking for his money. She went to the door with her purse in her hand.

It was a girl. She had Teddy in her arms.

"I brought your Teddy back, Mrs Zest," she said. "Jimmy sold it to me for an egg box."

Mrs Zest took the Teddy and gave it a hug. "He's a bad rascal," she said about her son. "He had no business selling it. It's very good of you to give it back."

"We think he's a genius, Mrs Zest," she said.

*

Without any doubt, that Friday was one of the great days in the life of James Zest.

At half past eight in the morning he opened the garage door and wheeled it out into the light of day – his model dinosaur, eight foot high and every inch as long.

Such a sight! You had to admire that egg box wonder. The main body rested on a set of pram wheels and, to make it even easier to push, there was a small wheel on its tail. As it glided down the drive, higher than the highest hedge, it looked like something from the beginning of time.

To get it out on to the main road, Jimmy Zest had to stop the traffic. Shorty and Legweak, who had been invited to help, pulled on a rope, and Penny Brown pushed.

The dinosaur was on its way – to school.

The sight of an eight foot dinosaur on its way to school was bound to attract a crowd. People came in all shapes and sizes, offering to help. "Want a hand, Zesty?" they shouted, and whether Zesty wanted a hand or not, he got plenty.

So many came that they formed a procession. The grocer came to the door of his shop to see it pass. So did Mr Buckley, the butcher. As people drove by in their cars they sounded their horns at

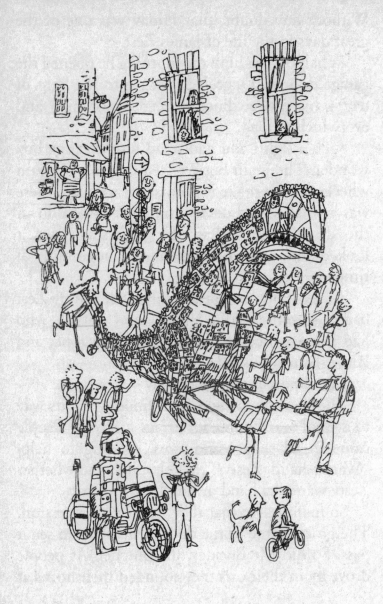

the wonderful sight of a dinosaur sailing along in the middle of a crowd

As the procession turned up the hill to the school a policeman on a motorcycle came by to see what all the fuss was about.

"What's going on here, then?" he wanted to know. "Where are you going with that there monster?"

Jimmy Zest stepped out of the crowd. "It's part of my dinosaur project, Sir. I'm taking it to school."

"Are you going to teach it to read?"

Jimmy Zest heard voices as he pushed.

"That's him in the brown jumper."

"There he goes, Jimmy Zest."

"It's an egg box wonder."

"That's our school genius, you know."

"Maybe we'll get a half day."

Jimmy Zest felt very proud. At the top of the hill he saw the headmaster and some of the teachers waiting for him.

The headmaster was very puzzled by the whole thing. Jimmy Zest could understand that perfectly.

"It's a surprise, Sir," he explained, "I'm giving it to the school – free."

"What the devil is it?" the headmaster asked,

and gave a signal for the school bell to be rung. It was ten past nine already.

At break-time, there wasn't a teacher to be seen about the school. They were all at a meeting in the headmaster's office.

The headmaster did the talking. "Well, this is an historic day, ladies and gentlemen of the staff. As I'm sure you know, James Zest has presented the school with a dinosaur."

There was a lot of laughter at this. Somebody asked, "It won't go through the door of a classroom. What are we going to do with it?"

Some of the suggestions were not very nice.

The headmaster said, "James Zest thinks it should go in the school canteen. He says it's a meat-eating dinosaur."

There was a lot more talk about Jimmy Zest's egg box wonder, and a lot more laughter. But in the end they agreed to let it stand in a corner of the school canteen – for one week.

– 2 –
The Thing in the Garden

One day after school Penny Brown took a risk. She walked home with Knuckles and Shorty.

Knuckles was not like his brother. Shorty was tough, but he hardly ever hit people – only when he lost his temper, which wasn't often. Knuckles lost his temper all the time and hit people for no reason at all, especially Shorty. Only once before in her whole life had Penny Brown walked home with Knuckles, and she'd been a nervous wreck. He had tried to thumb a lift down the school hill in a *teacher*'s car, and had got them chased when he threw a tin of shandy into a woman's garden. She hoped that his behaviour would be better today.

They were talking about the holidays and where they were going to spend them. In Penny Brown's opinion, Spain sounded like a very boring place. The grown-ups only went there to lie on the beaches and let the sun drain every ounce of energy out of them. Shorty said Disney Land must be a great place. When it came to his turn, Knuckles simply said, "Hong Kong."

"That's very far away, Knuckles," Penny Brown pointed out.

"All the same, it must be some place, that Hong Kong. Listen, you pick up any toy and turn it upside down and look at it and what do you see? 'Made in Hong Kong'. They can make anything over there."

"Mandy Taylor says she's going to Italy."

"I pity them," said Knuckles.

"Either Italy or Greece. She says the sun there would tan you to a crisp."

"Maybe they'll put her in salt and vinegar and eat her," said Knuckles hopefully. Mandy Taylor was not his favourite person. Then he started to pick a brick out of a stone wall.

Penny walked quickly ahead, thinking how this sort of thing showed exactly the difference between the twins: Shorty got up on walls and walked on them, but Knuckles picked out bricks and made them fall down.

Soon they came to a tall and very forbidding wooden fence along the edge of the pavement. A thick laurel hedge peeped over the fence like an extra barrier, and this hedge, with the help of a few sycamore trees, threw the entire section of pavement into cool shadow. Over that fence was the very private garden of Mrs Cricklewood-Holmes.

Penny knew very little about Mrs Cricklewood-Holmes – only that she was very rich; and that she kept Dobermann dogs; and that her son's picture had been in the paper a few years ago because he had a pet falcon. It was impossible to see into her garden because of the fences on all sides, and the sycamores were too high even for human monkeys like Knuckles to climb. Then Penny saw what she didn't want to see. Knuckles had found that one of the planks in the fence was swinging loose.

"Oh no, Knuckles," she said, "please don't go in there. Not Cricklewood-Holmesy's garden, she's a millionaire for goodness' sake!"

She might as well have talked to the nearest lamp post, for Knuckles was not the sort to pass up the chance of a quick nose around a private garden, especially one owned by a millionaire. After a glance up and down the street he went in through the dark hole.

"Don't *you* go, Shorty," Penny said, but too late.

Shorty's voice reached her from the other side

of the fence, saying, "It's OK, we're just looking for bonfire wood. We're not after her money."

With her mind made up not to get involved, Penny began to walk on. Then she heard a couple of stifled yells, some scuffling, and the furious rustling of branches. Shorty and Knuckles came panicking through the hole in the fence and fell in a heap on the pavement.

Penny ran to help them, but they were in such a state that they didn't even see her. Shorty's eyes had grown huge, Knuckles opened and shut his mouth like a fish looking for water. Then they took off down the road at a speed which Penny could not possibly match.

Penny Brown took a long, hard look at the hole behind the swinging plank and wondered whether she ought to go through it. She nearly did – until she looked to see where the twins had gone and found that they were already out of sight. She decided that it wasn't worth the risk when she would hear all about it tomorrow. Anyway – probably it was only a dog.

But Penny Brown was wrong. The Thing in Cricklewood-Holmesy's garden was definitely not a dog.

That same evening, as Mrs Zest was trying to get her son James away from the television set and up to his bed, there was a knock at the front door. When she answered it there stood two boys with curly, red hair – the Alexander twins. They had a bag of chips with them. The smell of vinegar from the soggy paper made Mrs Zest wrinkle up her nose.

The one called Shorty spoke first. "Hello, Missus. Is Zesty coming out?"

"Hello, Shorty, I think you're the one I know. I take it this is your brother?"

"Yeah, Knuckles. We've got news for Zesty."

"Oh? What's that?"

"Uh-uh. It's a secret."

"Well in that case I'll get James for you."

Between them, Knuckles and Shorty put together the story of what they'd seen in Cricklewood-Holmesy's garden: how the Thing appeared out of nowhere and stood on the grass looking all around it, "smelling the wind", as Shorty put it. It was so big, they said, that it couldn't get through Zesty's front door without bending double. And the head on it! That big black head with no eyes, no nose, no mouth. Shorty shuddered to think of it, then fed his face a chip.

"Was it a sort of phantom?" Jimmy Zest prompted.

"What's that?"

"Like a ghost. Something that wasn't there."

"It was there all right," said Knuckles, "big and straight and stiff and with this big, black head. It was Anti-human."

"Anti-human?"

"That's what I call it – the Anti-human."

"Was it carrying anything?"

"Certainly. It had a sort of a gun thing tucked in here, under its elbow."

"So it had arms?"

50

"And legs," said Shorty. "It walked from side to side like this," – he went on a tour of the hall – "as if it had no knees. I've never seen anything like it before, Zesty. It was like . . . like . . ."

"Anti-human," Knuckles finished gravely.

Jimmy Zest stood under the light in the hall looking thoughtful, as if he might have an idea what this Thing was.

"We'll take a look at it," he said.

"*Now*?" The terror flared in Shorty's eyes at the thought of seeing that monster in the gloom.

"No, not now. Some day after school."

As Knuckles left, he said very seriously, "Not a word, Zesty, not a word. This is secret."

Penny Brown sat beside the twins through dinners. It wasn't a nice experience, for neither Knuckles nor Shorty liked to waste time talking when there was food about. They shovelled potatoes into their mouths as if their elbows were mechanical diggers, and they were up for seconds before some people had sat down with their firsts. Penny wondered whether the pair of them would come to school at all if it wasn't for the dinners.

She asked, for the third time, "What did you see in Cricklewood-Holmesy's garden?"

No answer came. Only the sound of them guzzling other people's left-over prunes.

Outside in the playground they were worse. Knuckles kept making quiet remarks about phantoms and spacemen and Anti-humans, and Shorty declared that the whole Earth might be in danger.

"What's the matter with you two?" Penny demanded when she lost patience. "You're acting as if I'm not even here. Shorty, *you* tell me – what did you see in Cricklewood-Holmesy's garden? Bet it was only a snook of a dog."

Shorty looked at Knuckles, who said they might as well tell her if she swore never to pass the information to any other living human being. "Especially not Mandy Taylor," added Knuckles.

Penny Brown closed her eyes and swore.

"Well," Shorty began, "we saw a phantom, or a

spaceman, we don't know which. Big gloves it had, and no face. I call it the Thing, Knuckles says it's Anti-human and the whole Earth could be in danger."

"Such rubbish," said Penny Brown.

Knuckles held up his left hand very seriously.

"You see that hand? I swear by my left hand that no human being should go into Cricklewood-Holmesy's garden alone."

"What's so special about your left hand?"

"All left hands are special, the veins go straight to your heart."

At that moment Jimmy Zest came round the corner with Gowso and Legweak. Penny rushed off to find Mandy Taylor so that they could talk over this latest piece of news before afternoon lessons.

Of course she'd promised not to tell. On the other hand, if there was evil in that garden, people ought to know about it for their own safety.

They were very solemn, and very quiet, as they stood before the swinging plank in the fence that guarded Cricklewood-Holmesy's garden. Nervously, Mandy Taylor twisted the thin gold ring on her little finger as she said, "Do you really think we ought to go in?"

Penny Brown touched the swinging plank and

looked a little disappointed that it hadn't been fixed.

"I'll go in if you go in," she whispered.

"What'll we say if we're caught?"

"Say we lost our ball."

"Oh, Penny, ought we to go in?"

They stood arguing on the pavement like a couple of cowards and finally squeezed through together.

They squatted in the bushes and peered through the laurel leaves. At first nothing stirred, only a startled bird or two. Mandy pointed to a row of tiny houses at the end of the garden, little wooden houses with roofs on, as if Cricklewood-Holmesy kept fairies at the bottom of her garden as well as Dobermann dogs and falcons. Penny had no idea

what the tiny houses were for, and very soon she didn't care – Cricklewood-Holmesy's phantom was coming down the path in broad daylight!

Mandy began to shake as it came closer to their hiding place. The big, black head kept turning from side to side as if the Thing knew somebody was watching it. Something like a claw dug into Penny's upper arm and made her jerk with fear, but it was only Mandy taking a reassuring hold.

"Ohhh!" said Mandy Taylor.

Penny stood up as the creature passed. She'd seen a film once about these Anti-humans that landed from outer space and took over human bodies from their owners and, unless she was very much mistaken, they looked exactly like this Thing in Cricklewood-Holmesy's garden. As it fiddled with its gigantic gloves, Penny Brown wondered what kind of hands it must have.

"It's got a *green* gun!" she whispered hoarsely to Mandy, and got the shock of her life.

Mandy wasn't there.

Within seconds, neither was Penny. After a dash to the fence she shot through the hole and saw Mandy waiting for her across the road. "Mandy, what *was* that monster?" said Penny Brown as they made their way home down the safer side of the street.

It was three-thirty the following day. A small group of people had gathered around the school gate and were talking fiercely among themselves, for the secret was out. There was something very peculiar about Cricklewood-Holmesy's garden.

"In my opinion," said Gowso, "it sounds like one of the Undead."

"Can't be," said Legweak.

"Could be," said Mandy Taylor, shivering. "A sort of walking corpse with its face eaten away by worms."

"Nope. Corpses only walk at night."

"Why's that?" asked Shorty.

"They can't stand the sun," explained Legweak.

Penny Brown's voice was not quite normal. "Yesterday was a cloudy day. There wasn't any sun!"

Legweak said he thought it sounded like a mechanical gardener with stiff legs – a sort of robot. Probably it clanked as it walked.

Knuckles turned to Jimmy Zest, who hadn't said much. "What do you think, Zesty?"

Jimmy Zest stood with his thumbs tucked comfortably under the straps of his old-fashioned schoolbag. "I think we should all go and take a look at it."

This idea was eagerly received by Legweak. "Then if it attacks us we can all jump on it. There's seven of us."

"Fair enough," said Knuckles responsibly. "Everybody stay together and do what I tell them." As the discoverer of the Anti-human he felt obliged to take charge. After a hard look at Gowso, who was known to cry easily, he added, "And we don't want any weaklings."

Then they all headed off to see the Thing in Cricklewood-Holmesy's garden.

One by one they disappeared through the hole in the fence, Knuckles first, and Shorty, then Mandy and Penny, Legweak and Gowso and, finally, Jimmy Zest.

It was dark behind the fence, and cool beneath the shade of the huge leaves of sycamore. In a loud whisper Knuckles warned them not to leave the shelter of the laurel bushes or they would be seen and turned into a puff of smoke by the Anti-human's green weapon. They were a highly excited bunch of people hiding in the laurel bushes. Jimmy Zest sat on his schoolbag to wait for the action. Gowso climbed a tree and Mandy shrieked when Legweak tramped her hand into the dirt.

"Shhh!" Knuckles hissed.

Beyond the shadows of the bushes was a large, rectangular lawn all freshly mown and bathed in cloudy sunlight. The borders round the garden were thick with masses of shrubs and flowers. At the far end of the path, on a higher level than the lawn, stood the house itself. It had bulging bay windows on the ground and first floors. On the second floor many nooks and crannies had been built into the outer shell and there was even an interesting window in the roof. For observing the stars, Jimmy Zest guessed. No doubt about it, this was a very fine house. He could quite believe that Cricklewood-Holmes had a million pounds in the bank.

At the other end of the lawn the garden stopped at a wall grown over with creepers gone wild. Along the wall was a row of little houses with pointed roofs.

"Over there!" Knuckles whispered. They all looked to see where he was pointing.

Already the door of a small shed directly opposite them was opening and nobody could deny that each heart began to beat a little faster at what emerged from it.

It came walking forward in the stiff and awkward manner of a medieval knight, with its little green weapon firmly gripped in its enormous hands and with its great head looking too heavy by far for the shoulders that supported it.

Mandy Taylor got up on her knees. "Is it coming this way?"

"Sit still," said Legweak, who was trying to see over her head.

Penny Brown was on all fours. "I can't see its face, can you, Mandy?"

"No," said Gowso up the tree.

"It's *got* no face," Mandy declared in a horrified whisper. "How does it even breathe?"

Jimmy Zest heard scuffling and clattering in the branches above him and looked up in time to see Gowso making his escape along the arm of a sycamore tree and down on to the pavement outside. The Thing turned its triangular black face under a fantastic head-dress in the direction of the noise.

"It's seen us," Shorty shouted. "Run for it!"

As Mandy and Penny and Shorty went tearing for the hole in the fence, the creature began to shrill at them from the middle of the garden. By the time Jimmy Zest had gathered up his schoolbag and bolted after them he saw that it no longer mattered how much they hurried for they were all too late. A ferocious black Dobermann was in the gap, baring its teeth at them.

All they could do was wait while the Thing from the garden came closer. Mandy, who was very emotional, began to yell and Legweak began to whimper. Knuckles picked up the biggest stick he could find and looked as if he wasn't going to give in to an Anti-human without a fight. Shorty tried to look stupid, as if he was only there because he'd taken a wrong turning. Penny Brown wished that she was Gowso and Jimmy Zest's mind was working overtime.

With one menacing arm, the Thing motioned them out of the shadows and on to the lawn. The dog came after them, at their heels.

Now they saw a strange sight. The figure reached up and pulled a black veil from her face. Mandy Taylor, when she saw the natural, silvery hair, allowed her lungs to collapse in a great sigh of relief.

"Oh, you're human!" Penny Brown said with quiet passion, and the stick in the hands of Knuckles dropped a little lower.

The woman was in a raging temper. "You children have no business being here. What are you doing trespassing on my property? Be quiet!" she yelled at Penny Brown, whose mouth had opened to speak. "This is a private garden – isn't that right, Caligula?"

The dog, hearing its name, echoed the anger of his mistress with a fearful growl.

"What are *you* doing, boy?" Mrs Cricklewood-Holmes yelled at Jimmy Zest.

Jimmy had his schoolbag open and was busy handing out bits of paper to Shorty and the others, who were standing in a rather dejected line. Then he reached into the inside pocket of his jacket, where he had a battery of fifteen clip-on pens and pencils of one sort and another. He made sure that they had one each.

"Mrs Cricklewood-Holmes, we are doing research for our class project on animals. I wonder if we might ask you some questions about your bees?"

Knuckles took his eyes off Caligula and stared at the equally unfamiliar sight of a fountain pen with real ink in his hand.

"My bees? What do you know about bees?" snapped Mrs Cricklewood-Holmes.

"Down there," Jimmy Zest pointed at the little wooden houses, "those are your hives. We thought that perhaps . . ."

Penny Brown gave a little cough. She saw what was happening.

"We're very interested, Mrs Cricklewood-Holmes. Do you get stung often?"

"Why do you think I wear all this equipment? It keeps them off me when they start to buzz."

"The technical term is 'swarm', I believe," Jimmy Zest said. "I wonder what do you think of this new killer bee they've found in South America?"

"Killer bee my eye!"

Jimmy Zest leaned forward to look down the line. "Have you a question about bees, Shorty?"

"I dunno. How many has she?"

"What bees?" Knuckles said aggressively. "I can't see any bees."

In her prim and proper voice, Mandy Taylor asked sweetly: "How much honey do they give, Mrs Cricklewood-Holmes? We're awfully interested."

Mrs Cricklewood-Holmes seemed to like Mandy, the way all the teachers did. Perhaps it had something to do with her elocution classes.

"Well," she said, "I get enough to do me. But you people had no business coming in here."

"None at all," agreed Jimmy Zest.

"Don't come in here again."

"Never, Missus," said Shorty, still with an eye on Caligula.

"Caligula – away and lie down. Go on, away and lie down. We'll let them go – *this* time."

She refused to let them through the fence, but led them up a concrete path, round the house and out through a side gate. Shorty was the last one through the gate, where he stopped to put a final question which had nothing to do with bees.

"Missus – is it true that you're a millionaire?"

Penny Brown sighed. Knuckles pricked up his ears, for he was very interested in the answer. Mrs Cricklewood-Holmes clipped Shorty on the head and said, "Listen, boy, there's more than you would like to know the answer to that. Now don't come back, for I warn you – Caligula never forgets a face!"

Outside on the street, the six classmates agreed that it must be their lucky day. As Jimmy Zest collected in his pencils and pens, Knuckles said, "Hey – did any of you see her apple trees? She's got apple trees growing down in the far corner."

Penny Brown saw the gleam in his eye and read

the badness in his mind. "In the autumn," she said to Mandy Taylor on the way home, "he'll be back for those apples, you mark my words."

Mandy agreed. "I hope that big black dog's waiting for him," she said.

- 3 -

The Strong-stomach Contest

It was after school. Most of the teachers had gone home and the caretakers were busy in the classrooms with their buckets and brushes, getting the place tidy for the following day.

Miss Quick had not yet gone home. Neither had Nicholas Alexander. These two were discussing why Knuckles had not handed in a homework for two weeks.

"Even your brother Noel," said Miss Quick, talking quietly, "even Noel has handed in work to me. Now what's so special about you that *you* can be excused work which is attempted by everybody else?"

"I've been sick, Miss," said Knuckles.

"You have not been sick, you've been at school."

She didn't sound a bit angry with him. Some days she screeched at him and went red in the face so Knuckles figured that this must be one of her quiet days. Knuckles didn't understand teachers.

Miss Quick picked up her bag. "Well, I just want to tell you that I'm getting rather tired of struggling with you. What will you do, Nicholas, if people simply stop caring what you do or what becomes of you?"

"Dunno, Miss."

And then she said he could go. Knuckles dashed through the school buildings and grounds and out into the street just in case he could see Legweak or Zesty to walk home with, but it was far too late, thanks to Miss Quick. Even the patrol man and his big lollipop had gone home.

Knuckles decided to take the long way home, past the supermarket and through Elm Street. From Elm Street it would be easy to cut across the golf course to his own house. With a little bit of luck, he was thinking, he might pick up an empty bottle or two near the supermarket – once he'd got a refund of fifty pence for returning a huge cider bottle, the kind with a pair of funny glass ears. What a find that had been! Poor old Shorty had spent the next fortnight trying to find one, too.

There were no bottles of any kind to be seen today. Instead Knuckles found only trouble. The minute he turned into Elm Street and saw Maurice Baimes with his mates, he knew he was in bother.

There were three of them. The boy leaning against the gable of a house was Billy Parks. The one with the stick in his hand had a round body, round face and sticky-out ears. He was always called Gnome.

These two didn't worry Knuckles at all, for they were in his year at school. But Maurice Baimes was a different matter. He was older than Knuckles and had already left the primary school. Knuckles could remember as if it were yesterday the time he'd fought with Baimes in the playground during break. Neither of them had won because a teacher had come along and separated them. No doubt Baimes remembered, too.

"Forget your way home, Alexander?" he said. And he pushed himself off the gable wall in a very threatening way.

"I'm going through the golf course."

"No, you're not. That's our fence, *we* say who goes through it and who doesn't."

"Since when do you own the planet Earth, Baimes?"

"We'll let you through," said Baimes, "if you take a dead arm."

If you get hit hard enough in the right spot, your arm goes numb. Dead arm it's called. The thought of taking a dead arm from Baimes made Knuckles go hot with rage, but what else could he do? If he hit Baimes a smack on the mouth the three of them might start on him. On the other hand he had no intention of running away from them. People would soon get to hear about *that*.

Knuckles had bullied enough people to know that he had no choice. So he nodded his head once, and Baimes took him by the left arm.

"No," snapped Knuckles, "not that arm. Here." He held out his right one.

"What's the difference?" Billy Parks asked him.

"It's your blood. The veins in your left arm

come straight out of your heart, ask any doctor. I'm not taking a dead left arm."

Left arm, right arm — it didn't matter one bit to Maurice Baimes. He closed his fist into a ball and hit Knuckles a paralysing thump. Billy Parks and Gnome sniggered with delight as Knuckles winced in pain. Then they let him go.

He ran for the fence which separated Elm Street from the golf course, slung his schoolbag over the barbed wire, and began to climb. From the safety of the other side he turned and yelled at the other three: "I'll be back for you, Baimes!" And away he went across the golf course like a wounded hare, thinking how this was all Miss Quick's fault, and how he would round up Gowso and Legweak and Shorty and anybody else who would come and then they would see who gave whom a dead arm!

In no time at all the news of this latest piece of trouble between Knuckles and Maurice Baimes had reached everybody's ears. Shorty flew round to Jimmy Zest's house and then to Penny Brown's and she phoned up Mandy Taylor immediately. Then Legweak and Gowso arrived on one bike to meet up with the others at the shops.

They wanted all the details, of course. Knuckles was eating chips, which explained why his mouth steamed as he talked. "We're going to go round and see Maurice Baimes," he said. "Nobody gives me a dead arm for nothing. Somebody has to keep an eye on Billy Parks and Gnome, that's what you're here for. Can you fight, Gowso? What about you, Zesty?"

"Fight?" said Jimmy Zest, as if this was a new word he'd come across. Knuckles punched the air. "Fight. With your fists, like that."

Nobody had ever seen Jimmy Zest fighting. There was a general feeling that his talents lay in other directions, such as making money out of things which other people threw away. He was the kind of person who got out of trouble by using his tongue rather than his fists. Once in a blue moon he got really mad – as when somebody stole his giant dinosaur – but as a rule he was not one for getting into fights.

Nevertheless, he made it clear that he did not intend to miss this one.

"I'll come too," he said.

They were ready. As soon as Legweak had fastened the lock round a wheel of his bike the group moved off in the direction of Elm Street. Then Knuckles noticed Mandy Taylor.

"Where do you think you're going?"

"Elm Street," she said, not too fiercely.

70

"Not with us, you're not."

"She is so," said Penny Brown.

Knuckles took a swipe at Mandy Taylor and made her run away a few yards.

"It's a free country, Nicholas Alexander," roared Penny Brown. "We can go if we want and we do want – don't we, Mandy?"

Mandy didn't seem too sure, but Penny Brown pulled her by the arm.

"Come on, we'll link arms and stand our ground. Shorty doesn't mind if we come, do you, Shorty?"

This was a bit embarrassing for Shorty. Mandy Taylor had been a girlfriend of the dreadful Baimes and could therefore be called a bit of a traitor; on the other hand he did not like to offend Penny Brown . . .

It didn't matter. Impatient to be off, Knuckles was already striding away with Gowso and Legweak after him, then Jimmy Zest and Shorty. Bringing up the rear, at a safe distance and still with their arms linked, came the girls.

Their route took them past their school, which was all locked up for the night and completely deserted. Knuckles marched along at the front of his troops feeling like a general. It was a good thing that he couldn't hear what was being said about him at the very back.

"Look at him," said Penny Brown, "somebody should ring the zoo and tell them one of their cages is empty."

"I hope Maurice knocks his head in," whispered Mandy Taylor – which quite shocked Penny. Her friend was very polite and didn't often talk so roughly.

Then Mandy gave a little gasp as she and Penny turned into Elm Street and saw Maurice Baimes!

Had he been expecting them? It seemed so. He was standing by a lamp post with Billy Parks and Gnome and he looked a bit angry, or maybe even, worried.

"I'm not on my own now, Baimes," Knuckles shouted out. "Let's see how big you are now."

Shorty, who loved trouble better than his breakfast, shuffled with excitement as Baimes came forward. Gowso edged towards the back and Penny Brown noticed that Mandy did something very interesting. She moved away to the side as if she wasn't with Knuckles and his people at all.

Baimes took his hands out of his pockets. "Come on, then," he said to Knuckles.

"Come on yourself."

They stood glaring at one another. It seemed that the slightest movement would make one fly at the other.

"I don't think this is a very good idea," said a voice.

It belonged to Jimmy Zest, who stood there like a traffic warden talking to a naughty motorist. And Shorty wasn't a bit pleased with the interruption.

"What are you talking about, Zesty?"

"They're going to hurt each other, aren't they?"

"Well, it's a fight," Shorty pointed out.

"What's the sense in everybody ending up with black eyes? I've got a better idea. We should hold a strong-stomach contest."

This baffled everyone. Since nobody had a clue what he meant, Jimmy Zest went on, "Like a pie-eating contest, only instead of pies they have to eat something they don't like. Well . . . something revolting, actually. The one who eats most is the winner. It would be far more interesting."

There was almost complete silence. Somebody said "Flute" in the background and of course this was Penny Brown thinking out loud. Maurice Baimes appeared to be thinking over the idea and Knuckles asked, "What sort of stuff would we eat?"

"I'll pick the food," said Jimmy Zest. "It won't be very nice. In fact it will be horrible. It will take a very brave person to eat it. And there'll have to be rules, everybody can see that. I'll make the rules. We'll have the contest on Saturday morning on neutral ground. I suggest the golf course."

Shorty didn't like it, he was shaking his head. But the others were crowding round keenly. Mandy Taylor had gone right to the front – Penny suspected that she'd gone up there so that Maurice Baimes would speak to her.

"I'll do it if he will," said Baimes.

"Go on, Knuckles," shouted Gowso, and Penny Brown said, "You've got a good strong stomach, Knuckles."

She knew. She had watched him move mountains of food down his throat at dinners.

Knuckles grunted. "All right."

"Shall I make arrangements, then?" asked Jimmy Zest.

A frown had appeared on the brow of

Billy Parks. "How can we trust you, you're on their side."

"Jimmy Zest is a very fair person," said Penny Brown indignantly. "He could easily be a lawyer or a judge, isn't that right, Mandy?"

"That's right," replied Mandy sweetly.

Maurice Baimes looked long and hard at the impartial Jimmy Zest. Apparently reassured by what he saw, he nodded.

Jimmy Zest held up his hands to quieten the sudden buzz of excitement which had broken out.

"That's it, then," he declared officially, "Knuckles Alexander versus Maurice Baimes. There shall be a strong-stomach contest on the golf course – this Saturday morning."

But the next day was only Friday. They had a

whole day to wait. And on Friday morning a row broke out between Penny Brown and Mandy Taylor. It was about the strong-stomach contest.

"You want Baimes to win," shouted Penny Brown. "I dare you to deny it. We all know he's your boyfriend."

Mandy Taylor blushed. "He isn't."

"He was."

"He's not. And I don't want him to win, I want—" she had a problem now, for it was well known that she loathed Nicholas Alexander, "—I want it to be a draw."

"No chance," said Shorty, who knew what it was like to come up against Knuckles.

All the same Shorty became quite alarmed at dinner that Friday. Knuckles went up for seconds of apple crumble. Then he sent up a younger kid to fetch him thirds. In vain, Shorty tried to convince his twin that he ought to starve a little and so be ready for the big contest.

"Look," Knuckles told him, "this is only Friday. I've got to live in the meantime."

These small rows and minor worries were a sign that the strong-stomach contest had gripped the imagination of everyone who knew about it. And of course there was one big question which remained unanswered: what on earth would the contestants actually have to *eat*? Nobody knew but Jimmy Zest.

He disappeared at break-time, just when everybody wanted to torment him with questions. At lunch time he was spotted up an oak tree and he flatly refused to come down, saying that he was writing out the rules for the competition and would they please go away and leave him alone. Penny Brown was raging at him.

Only guessing was left.

"I thought of frogs," said Gowso. "Think about frogs – they're slimy, fat and squelchy. Couldn't be better."

"Yuk," said Legweak, but Penny Brown was nodding.

"Zesty said it would be horrible. Frogs are horrible. I thought of scallops. Have you ever eaten scallops? They are *rotten*, they taste like crab's toes."

"Never knew they had feet," said Shorty.

"Ooh," Mandy Taylor shivered, "imagine eating crab's toes."

"Well, Mandy, you don't think he'll dish up chocolate éclairs."

This made Mandy Taylor smile. The more horrible the food, the more chance there was that Nicholas Alexander would end up sick as a dog.

Ten minutes after the bell for the end of school, Jimmy Zest was jogging down Elm Street with some information in his pocket for Maurice Baimes. He had to wait a while since the secondary school got out twenty minutes later than the primary. It annoyed the methodical Jimmy Zest to have forgotten this, but he passed the time by studying the writing on the gable walls. The spelling of some of the words was wrong. He wondered whether people would pay him money to remove the writing. Methylated spirits might do the trick and it was cheap to buy. Then he heard someone saying his name. It was Maurice Baimes.

Jimmy Zest wasted no time in reaching into his pocket for a piece of paper.

"I have here the rules of the contest. Knuckles Alexander has already agreed to them. Would you like me to read them out?"

"Read away, Zesty."

"One. The contest shall begin at ten-thirty a.m. Two. The contest shall be held in the bunker behind the seventeenth hole."

At this point Billy Parks interrupted. "Where's that?"

"The pit with the sand in it – the one furthest away from the clubhouse. Three. The food shall

78

be eaten in turns, first mouthful to be decided by the toss of a coin. Four. The food shall be eaten raw."

Gnome, when he heard that, stuck out his tongue as far as it would go. Jimmy Zest ignored him. "Five. The food shall be sufficiently revolting for this to be a genuine test of a strong stomach."

"Talk English, Zesty."

"Six. Flavoured drinks like orange etcetera shall not be permitted. Jimmy Zest shall inspect water bottles. Seven. Jimmy Zest shall be sole judge and umpire. Eight – and finally – the loser shall agree to take a dead arm from the winner."

The folded paper returned to Jimmy Zest's hip pocket. "Do you agree?"

Gnome had suddenly become very excited. "What'll the food be, tell us?"

"Can't say."

It was Baimes who objected. "Bet you've told Alexander."

"No. Anyway, you're better not knowing. If I told you what you'll be eating you might be up all night, worrying."

This was a very good point. As Jimmy Zest headed off home Maurice Baimes was looking very thoughtful indeed.

*

It was a beautiful morning.

The sun shone out of a clear sky when the day of the contest dawned. By a quarter past ten Knuckles was leading his supporters into a stiff breeze blowing across the golf course. Gowso and Legweak came next with serious faces, then Shorty, and finally Penny Brown and Mandy Taylor, who had a woollen hat pulled down over her ears. She was busily complaining that her feet were getting wet with the dew.

"Well, you didn't have to come," Penny pointed out, rather harshly. She had a feeling at the back of her mind that Mandy might as well have stayed at home if she was only hoping for a draw.

Penny had another worry which she kept to herself. Jimmy Zest wasn't with them. What an awful thing it would be if the umpire didn't turn up.

She should have known better. The tactful Jimmy Zest, aware of the importance of his position, had decided that he ought to arrive by himself, before his friends, to show how fair he meant this contest to be.

And so, when the Alexander contingent arrived, they found Maurice Baimes already present with his supporters, and Jimmy Zest standing to one side, tapping his watch.

"You're late," he said snappily.

"We were waiting for *you*, Zesty," said Penny Brown, just as snappily.

"I am the umpire," Jimmy Zest reminded her. "Water bottles, please."

Shorty and Gnome brought lemonade bottles to the umpire, who unscrewed each cap and tasted what was inside. Satisfied that it was only water, he jumped into the sandy bunker and set a plastic container at his feet. The label said Ice Cream, but every single person guessed that this was the food, and that the food was not ice cream.

Jimmy Zest said, "Before we start we need a look-out. I appoint Gowso to be the look-out."

"Aw, Zesty!"

There was no argument. The umpire, backed up by other voices, forced Gowso away from the bunker to watch out for early morning golfers.

Then Jimmy Zest flicked a coin and stared hard at Maurice Baimes.

"Heads."

"Tails it is. Knuckles, do you want first mouthful or second?"

Knuckles jumped into the bunker and stared for a moment or two at the plastic container sitting in the sand. Through the plastic he could see the dark outline of a heap of things. He could

almost swear he saw them moving. So he pointed at Maurice Baimes.

"Knuckles Alexander won the toss," called the umpire. "Maurice Baimes will go first." Jimmy Zest peeled the lid off the container.

The audience stared in silence. Then, "Oh flute . . . !"

"They'd make you sick just looking."

"He must have got those out of his garden."

"He's going to make them eat . . ."

"Worms," said Jimmy Zest.

Worms. A well-scrubbed mass of pink and brown creatures, each with its long, thin body curled under, round and over lots of other pink and brown bodies in the plastic container. Each worm was moving just a little, with the result that the horrible heap seemed to writhe and heave.

"Yuk, Yuk! They're bound to be poison," muttered Gowso. Even Jimmy Zest forgot to remind him that he was supposed to be keeping look-out.

"Every stomach has acids," said Jimmy Zest. "These acids will attack the worms and digest them."

The word "cruelty" was spoken, which annoyed Shorty.

"It is not! Fishermen sticks hooks through them all the time."

"Away and ring the RSPCA," said Legweak, which some people thought was a good joke.

Jimmy Zest was in a serious mood, and he warned the spectators that it was time to start. They retreated from the sand, leaving the two contestants alone with their umpire: and all three looked very solemn. After waiting for complete silence – which wasn't long coming – Jimmy Zest held out the plastic container to Maurice Baimes.

The boy from Elm Street picked a worm from the pile and held it dangling between a finger and thumb. He had a most peculiar expression on his face. It was as if the worm had a bad smell and he was trying to block up his nose by using the muscles on his face. The trapped worm curled, grew extra thin and pink, except for the end which bulged, and grew darker.

"Get it in your mouth, Mo," cried a single voice. This was Gnome.

And Maurice Baimes did what he could to get the worm into his mouth. He swallowed his saliva and gulped and swallowed again and brought the worm to where it almost touched his teeth. Then he let it drop into the sand and walked away, saying, "I'm not eating that thing."

"Go on, Knuckles," cried a voice from the crowd.

This was Shorty, who knew that his twin must be hungry. Knuckles had skipped breakfast to be ready for this.

Without looking at what he was doing, Knuckles slid a worm from the heap in the plastic container. It seemed to go on for ever as its body slipped through all the others it had been curled around.

"One worm to win it, Knuckles," shouted Gowso.

Shorty was sweating, so he took a swig from his brother's water bottle. Legweak spat into the grass as he imagined the worm slipping down his throat like a strand of slippery onion. Legweak hated onions.

With his eyes shut now, as if he was praying, Knuckles had the worm dangling above his open mouth. He suddenly let go.

"Flute! He's got it in!"

The eyeballs in Knuckles's head began to fly as he tried to swallow. He began to hop about kicking up clouds of grit and uttering a sound like a dying man cleaning his teeth until, at last, he gave a panicking gulp, his body jerked forward and he gave a mighty retch.

Jimmy Zest, umpire, pointed at the second worm in the sand.

"He didn't swallow it!" yelled Baimes.

"I swallowed it, I swallowed it," screamed Knuckles – and bedlam occurred.

First of all, Billy Parks and Gnome pushed Gowso into the bunker when he declared that Knuckles had won it. Shorty clouted Gnome behind the knees and kicked sand in his eyes when he was down. Somebody passed Jimmy Zest with his hands up in the air as if he was signalling to an aeroplane pilot – this was Maurice Baimes calling "Draw! Draw!" And Baimes had Legweak talking to him, trying to explain that the worm had gone down into Knuckles's stomach and then come up again.

"Here's the greenkeeper!" yelled Penny Brown.

By now the sand was flying. Shorty, on his knees, had managed to get hold of both worms and was claiming that his brother's definitely looked as though it had been attacked by stomach acids. Meanwhile Jimmy Zest was already on his way home, for he had realized some time ago that Penny Brown was right – it *was* the greenkeeper.

The greenkeeper was in a rage: "You bunch of . . . Look at the state of my sand, my bunker, you bunch of hooligan pests, by all that's holy I'll sink my boot in the lot of you . . ."

The bunker was emptying fast. Shorty eluded a wild swipe from the greenkeeper's hand, which clouted Gnome instead. Mandy Taylor was standing there simply petrified by terror. All she could think of was how her daddy had belonged to the golf club until this moment. Now she would get him expelled.

"Run, you stupid!" yelled Knuckles as he passed her, running.

And Mandy ran too. She ran and ran until her lungs hurt, and she didn't stop running until she was absolutely certain that she'd escaped from the confusion which had put an end to the strong-stomach contest.

By Saturday afternoon Knuckles had become a bit of a hero. Even Mandy Taylor had to admit what a disgustingly brave thing it had been – to actually put a worm into your *mouth*.

They were all sitting on the wall at the shops, sucking ice lollies.

"You haven't said much, Zesty," said Penny Brown.

"Doesn't matter any more," came the reply.

"Oh, but it does matter, Zesty, we've all said what we think."

"And you were the umpire," Shorty added wisely.

Carefully, Jimmy Zest nipped the tip off his ice lolly with his front teeth.

"I'd like to know where you got all those worms," Gowso said.

"In my garden. You squirt washing-up liquid into the ground, that makes them come up. And Knuckles didn't win."

Penny Brown stared round her, to make sure that Knuckles wasn't there to hear this. Fortunately he was away with Legweak pulling sticks out of hedges or something.

"He didn't swallow that worm," Jimmy Zest continued, "or if he did, he didn't keep it down. That doesn't prove he's got the strongest stomach – only that he can take a worm into his mouth. Sorry, Shorty."

Shorty didn't mind. He knew it didn't matter what the umpire thought: Mo Baimes was due a dead arm and he was going to get one, probably on Monday.

- 4 -

Legweak the Stuntman

One day in class Legweak turned red as a beetroot.

It happened when Miss Quick was handing back the homework books. "Now, I had one really excellent piece of writing this time," she said. "It was quite the best work I've received from this boy and I'm going to read it out."

Of course, nobody knew yet that she was talking about Legweak. Several people began to make guesses. Knuckles turned right round in his seat and said he'd bet ten pounds that it was Zesty. Shorty said from the back of the room he'd bet ten pounds that it wasn't Knuckles – which made Penny Brown giggle out loud.

This is what Miss Quick read out: "My ambition is to be a stuntman in films or television. My dad thinks I'll change my mind but I've wanted to be a stuntman since last year. People don't realize that you have to work hard to make your ambitions come true. I practise every day on my bike. It's a very good bike. It's got hydraulic front suspension and four gears and dirt track tyres. I can jump three people when they are lying down. I think I could probably do six people if I had a proper ramp. That is my ambition."

Even if Legweak hadn't turned the colour of a beetroot, they would all have known that this was bound to be his homework. Anybody who'd ever seen him on a bike had to admit that he had a lot of class.

"That was very good, Stephen," Miss Quick told him – she never called him Legweak – "since yours was the best homework you can help me with the War Table today."

This made them all sit up. Even Knuckles tidied his desk and folded his arms like an angel. At the front of the classroom there was a table on which Miss Quick displayed objects of interest. She kept tadpoles there in the spring and in the autumn you could hardly see it for dead leaves. This table now had a label on it:

**OBJECTS FROM THE
SECOND WORLD WAR.**

Miss Quick asked Legweak to pick up an object from the War Table. He chose a knife with an enormous blade nearly half a metre long and with a dangerous point at one end.

"Careful, Stephen, it's a bayonet. If you were a soldier in the war you fitted this to your rifle and it became a kind of sword. Can you see why people talk about 'cold steel'?"

In the light coming through the window, the bayonet sparkled. Penny Brown shivered at the thought of it passing through a body.

"Was it pulled out of a dead German, Miss?" asked Knuckles.

Miss Quick sighed to hear this bloodthirsty question.

"No, Nicholas, it wasn't pulled out of anyone, I hope."

"Were you in the war, Miss?" asked a nice voice.

"I was just a little girl at school, Mandy, younger than you are. In those days we had brick shelters in the grounds of the school. Does anyone know why?"

Jimmy Zest's hand went up so quickly that he came slightly out of his seat. However, he was just beaten by Shorty, who answered, "For your bikes, Miss."

Jimmy Zest's hand stayed up. "To protect you from falling bombs, Miss."

"Yes. Although no bombs ever fell on us. Now let me remind you to ask your grandparents if they have any objects from the war which we could display on our table. We promise to take good care of them – don't we, Nicholas?"

They had Spanish meatballs for lunch. Knuckles told Mandy Taylor that when bull fighters killed the bulls in faraway Spain, the bulls weren't wasted: they were turned into meatballs and sent to the British Isles.

"Don't believe him, Mandy," warned Penny Brown, "he's just trying to sicken you so that he can get yours."

After lunch the boys drifted away to watch Legweak doing wheelies on his new bike. Penny and Mandy were not much interested in watching somebody riding around with one wheel in the air. A bike was a thing with two wheels and they could not see the point in making it go on just one. It was like being a human and having to hop around on one leg all the time.

They were more interested in the diagram which Jimmy Zest was scraping on the ground with a stick. "Enjoying yourself, Zesty?" asked Mandy Taylor.

She was ignored. Jimmy Zest added an arrow to his diagram in the dust and talked to Gowso. "If we had a ramp just there, the bike would take off into the air if Legweak was travelling at a good speed."

Gowso wasn't convinced. "There aren't any ramps like that round here, Zesty."

"We could build one. All we need are a few shovels and spades."

Gowso still wasn't convinced, but he whistled the others over to hear what they thought about this idea. Legweak got off his bike to peer closely at the ground.

"Where would we build this ramp?"

"The park, after tea. I'll draw a plan and we can do it tonight."

The thought of actually doing the stunt made Legweak ring the bell of his bike furiously, which got Gowso so excited that he yelled at the top of his voice, "Legweak's going to go for six people!"

Shorty swore it would be a world record.

And so, after tea, shovels and spades were taken up and carried to the park and, in a suitable place behind the bandstand, Jimmy Zest spread on the ground the plan he had drawn up for the construction of a ramp.

"Now," he said, pointing, "that thick line – that's the slope we're standing on. That shaded-in bit is what we're going to add on. That's the ramp. Legweak should be able to fly off it. Pile the soil in behind that plank."

He sounded most convincing. Nobody paid the slightest attention when Mandy Taylor asked if they had permission to go digging up the public park. Shorty had a bag of Liquorice All-Sorts with him which he now shared out, starting with Penny Brown and ending with Mandy Taylor; then they got stuck in. Jimmy Zest made them build a nice flat bit jutting out from the slope. They all stamped on the soil to make sure that it was firm. Then Jimmy Zest nodded to Legweak.

It was time for a trial run.

Legweak's new bike gleamed at the top of the slope. They could just see the determination on his face which was screwed up as if he found it painful to concentrate. The bike rocked to and fro.

"Vroom! Vroom!" said Gowso, making motorbike noises. "Come on, Legweak – go!"

Up went Legweak on one pedal, and away. His hair streamed back from his forehead as he gathered speed down the slope and you could hardly see his feet the way they whizzed the pedals round.

"You'd wonder how he does it," said Penny Brown, "he's got legs like matchsticks."

At the last possible moment, as his front wheel hit the ramp, Legweak came out of his crouching position low in the saddle and threw his weight forward into space.

It was a disaster. The front wheel of his bike ploughed a furrow through the freshly dug earth and knocked the plank flat. The bike didn't get off the ground – but Legweak did. He performed a terrifying loop in the air and tumbled to the bottom of the slope where he lay absolutely still.

The first to react to this awful event was Penny Brown, who said, "Oh, flute!" and ran to see if Legweak was OK. Shorty came next. By the time Mandy Taylor arrived with Jimmy Zest, Legweak was up on his feet and hobbling back up the slope.

Shorty shoved a grubby bag under his nose. "Here, Legweak – take an All-Sort."

Legweak had no time for All-Sorts. His poor bike was lying across the destroyed ramp with its front wheel still spinning. It looked like a stricken insect. Legweak closed an eye and inspected the front wheel for a buckle.

"Seems to be all right," he said.

Now that the danger was over, everyone started to put their point of view. Mandy Taylor was first.

"I thought he was dead. What did you think when you saw him lying there, Penny?"

Shorty said, "If that hadn't been a trial run, just think, we'd all have been crushed."

Penny Brown put the same thought another way. "Oh very *good*, Zesty, Legweak did a world-record *somersault*!"

The disconcerted Jimmy Zest stared humbly at the remains of his unsuccessful ramp and shook his head forlornly, as if here at last was something which he did not understand.

The attic in Jimmy Zest's house was reached by way of a trapdoor in the bathroom ceiling. His parents didn't allow him up the narrow homemade stairs on his own, so he had to ask their permission to go up and see if there was anything left over from the war.

His father took him through the trapdoor just before bedtime. The sun had been beating down on the roof all day long, with the result that Jimmy Zest found it hard to breathe in the still and stifling air of the roof space. His father warned him to be careful with his feet – it was very easy up here to put a foot wrong and go through a ceiling.

While his father sat on the rafters smiling at old photographs, Jimmy Zest went on the prowl among the piles of junk – stuff like old furniture, old plates, huge and heavy old records. Every item seemed to belong to an earlier age and of course this made sense. Anything of any use wouldn't be stuck up here at the top of the house and out of the way.

He found an old-fashioned razor. "Ah-ah," his father snapped, "put that down, it would cut the fingers off you. Look over there beside the water tank and you'll see something from the war."

It was a big, brass shell case, which his dad said had been fired at the Battle of El Alamein. Jimmy Zest had never heard of that. Then his father told him to open a huge cardboard box if he wanted to see something interesting.

It was a heavy thing to lift. The thing in the box seemed almost as big as himself and turned out to be a helmet of some kind, but made of rubber and canvas. On the front it had a panel of clear plastic stuff for a person inside to see out, and hanging down one side of it, like an elephant's trunk, was a floppy tube.

Jimmy Zest couldn't even guess what it was. "Put it on," his dad said.

The helmet came right over his shoulders and down to his waist. It was hard to breathe in there because the smell of the rubber caught in his nose. His father began to pump the elephant's trunk and on the inside Jimmy Zest could feel air blowing his hair about.

He took it off.

"Was it a gas mask?"

"Yes. But this one is a bit different from the ones you usually see. It was for your grandmother."

This was puzzling, for Jimmy Zest knew that his granny had been born during the war. "You mean . . . this was for babies?"

His father explained. During an air raid or a gas attack you were supposed to put your baby into this helmet thing with its legs sticking out. Of course, it couldn't breathe in there, so somebody outside – the baby's mum or dad – had to pump the dangling trunk and give it air. The strong metal frame which made the mask so heavy protected the baby from damage.

Jimmy Zest found this a horrifying thought.

"Was Granny ever put into that when she was small?" he asked as they came down the ladder.

His dad told him no, it wasn't ever needed.

The following afternoon this short note was passed round the class. It was signed by Jimmy Zest. Gowso read it first:

> *Another attempt at the world record tonight. After tea in the park. Pass it on.*

Gowso shook his head as if to say, "Who are you kidding, Zesty?" but he passed the message on. Penny Brown also wrote a note and passed it round the class. It said that Jimmy Zest had a nerve to go risking Legweak's neck twice in two days.

But they all turned up after tea in the park, just to see what would happen. And *this* time, the others were not so easy to convince.

Jimmy Zest had a new diagram with him, which he spread out for them all to see.

"I know what went wrong," he said confidently,

"the ground last time was too soft, that's all. This time we'll take the soil away instead of adding it on. See that shaded-in bit? We'll dig that out of the slope and make a ramp that way. This time Legweak'll be taking off from the slope itself. Do you see the difference?"

They saw the difference, certainly. But not one of them had any enthusiasm for this new plan – except Legweak, who could hardly wait to get going. After a few wheelies to warm up and some chat about which gear to put the bike into, he brought his machine to a halt at the top of the slope. The bike rocked to and fro, Legweak spat on both palms, and then he was suddenly away, raking down the slope with both feet whirling and his hair flowing in the wind.

When the bike left the ramp, Legweak stayed with it in the air. His machine and he hit the ground together – but they stayed upright and after correcting a fierce wobble, Legweak bounced back in the saddle and skilfully eased his machine into a sliding skid.

"Flute!" said Penny Brown. "He actually did it!"

A cheer broke out, Gowso yelled that they were home and dry as if *he* had been the one to make the jump, and Knuckles and Shorty took off in the wake of the victorious Legweak, who was riding about with one arm raised in a salute.

Now the excitement really began to mount. Everybody except Mandy Taylor agreed to lie down under the ramp and be jumped.

"But that ground's filthy," said Mandy Taylor.

"Mandy, you're not dressed for church," Penny Brown pointed out. "You've got your old clothes on, that's what they're *for*."

That settled that. Then they ran into a real problem, a giant-sized problem. None of them would volunteer to take the last place in the line. It was Shorty who pointed out that if Legweak's back wheel came down a bit short, you might get your ribs bashed in.

They stood in a group desperately trying to surmount this final obstacle. Gowso came up with an idea first.

"We could use a pillow for the last place.

If Legweak jumps a bit short he'll just hit the pillow."

Mandy Taylor retorted, with great authority, "A pillow? Whose mother would allow a pillow out of its bedroom to take part in this carry-on?"

Knuckles suggested, "We could get one of those fake people out of a shop window. It wouldn't matter about his ribs."

"We could leave a space," said Jimmy Zest.

Legweak was almost crying with indignation. "What kind of a world record would *that* be? What would people say if I jumped over five people and a *space*? Or five people and a dummy out of a shop?"

Penny Brown didn't let him get away with that. "It's all right for you, Legweak. What if you landed on somebody's throat? They'd never speak again."

Nobody was taking any chances. What they needed was an incredibly silly and incredibly brave person to risk being smashed up by Legweak's new bike – and they didn't have one.

A gloomy silence fell over them all until Jimmy Zest spoke. He asked Legweak to lend him his bike.

"I'll be back in seven minutes," he said. "I'll do it – I'll take the last place in the line."

He was
away for over
ten minutes,
actually; and
when he
returned the
others could
hardly believe
it was him.
Across the park
on Legweak's
machine came this creature which looked as if it
had just cycled in from the moon. All they could
see of Jimmy Zest was his eyes staring out from
the depths of the massive helmet with the metal
frame.

Shorty walked round Zesty for a rear view
of this monster, and saw some writing on the
back.

"It says here 'Government Property'."

Jimmy Zest came out from under his headgear.
"It was a gas mask for babies during the war. If
Legweak lands on this I won't get hurt."

Now they were all in business. First Shorty lay
down in the line, then Knuckles. Once again
Mandy Taylor threatened the operation when she
said: "I'm not lying down beside *him*."

She meant Knuckles, so the twins changed places to let her be beside Shorty, the lesser of two evils. Then Penny Brown stretched herself out, and Gowso, then Jimmy Zest at the end of the line with his huge mask on.

There they lay, face down, six heads pointing to the north and twelve feet pointing south, waiting to be jumped by Legweak on a bike.

Mandy Taylor wriggled between Shorty and Penny Brown. "I feel like a sardine."

"You look like a sardine." This was Shorty.

"You smell like a sardine." This was Knuckles.

"If she's a sardine, Nicholas Alexander, you're a squid," snapped Penny Brown. "Hurry up, Legweak and get this over with."

They couldn't hear him as they lay there waiting. The wind carried the sound of traffic from the direction of town. Then they heard the zing of Legweak's tyres in the short grass.

"Flute!" said Penny Brown. "Here he comes!"

She was thinking how this was what it must be like for insects when there were humans about. She shut her eyes and tried to think of something else entirely when all of a sudden she heard a terrible clatter and an awful yell and her first thought was that Jimmy Zest had been chopped in two.

The line broke up in confusion. Jimmy Zest whipped his helmet off his head and knelt down beside Gowso to find out what was the matter with him.

"I . . . can't . . . get air," Gowso was saying. He had a panic-stricken expression on his face and his eyes bulged like ping-pong balls.

Legweak's jump had gone wrong. He hadn't even reached Jimmy Zest. The rear wheel had come down on Gowso's back and left a mark – as they saw when they rolled up his shirt to inspect him for damage. Already he had a sore, red bruise.

Soon, though, they had him sitting up and breathing more easily, and there was no need for the ambulance which Mandy Taylor had immediately called for. Shorty forced a brandy-ball into Gowso's mouth and within a minute he was up on his feet.

"That's the *last* time, Zesty," swore Penny Brown.

The miserable Legweak came over with the front lamp of his bike in his hands. It had broken off.

"Sorry about that, Gowso. I got nervous when I saw you all lying there. I fluffed it."

Gowso waved a hand as if it didn't matter.

But it did matter. Penny Brown, anxious to pin the blame for this shambles on as many people as possible, declared, "Yes. Well next time, Legweak, I advise you to jump pillows and leave people out of it."

- 5 -

Jimmy Zest Mind-slaves, Ha, Ha, Ha

Penelope Brown was curious.

Miss Quick had asked her class to bring along an item for the Science table – anything at all really, so long as it was useful to the human race. They were learning about MATERIALS.

What would people bring to school? Penny wanted to take her mother's beautiful, hand-painted, Japanese silk fan, but her mother said Most Definitely Not, and so Penny had to make do with a clay pot.

At the school gates she met Gowso nursing a plastic bread-bin. Legweak was there too, wearing a blue rope like a sash. "This rope is made of synthetic fibre, you know," he said proudly as the Alexander twins arrived. "What did you bring, Shorty?"

"Who, me?" said Shorty, as if there were ten other Shortys close by.

"We forgot," said Knuckles.

"It was your *homework* to bring in something for the Science table," Penny Brown pointed out; but those twins didn't care two hoots about little things like that. They stood there empty-handed without a worry in the world.

Then Jimmy Zest arrived. "I brought diamonds," he said.

Absolutely typical, thought Penny Brown. No clay pots or plastic bins for Mr Jimmy Zest. Surely he hadn't brought his mother's precious engagement ring to school?

Just then a fancy car drew up and Mandy Taylor struggled out with a cardboard box that was quite a bit longer than herself. The boys stared at it, growing more and more curious by the moment.

"Well?" said Mandy. "Do you see enough? Ask no questions and you'll be told no lies. And you can't eat it, Nicholas Alexander, so hard luck."

As soon as he heard the word "eat", Knuckles's face lit up and he zoomed off towards the caretaker's house. Then the hurry-bell rang and the others trotted into the playground to line up. At the classroom door a somewhat breathless Knuckles caught up with them, and in his hand was a bone: a huge, shiny, white bone, well chewed around the edges. The sight of it made

Penny Brown and Mandy Taylor look at one another, for they knew that he must have pinched it from the caretaker's dog. Did he really expect animal remains to sit on the MATERIALS table?

"How is *that* useful to the human race?" asked Penny Brown.

"Making soup."

At that moment Gowso leaned forward and tapped Mandy's box with a long finger. "That's a knitting machine," he said.

"It's not," said Mandy.

"It is," said Gowso.

"It *isn't*."

"My auntie's knitting machine came in a box like that."

"Philip McGowan," said Penelope Brown, "Mandy and I know what this is and it's not a knitting machine and if you keep on saying it *is* a knitting machine then your head is full of fungus."

That was when Miss Quick, with truly sickening timing, opened her classroom door. She believed very strongly in things like fresh air and speaking nicely to people. Even people like Gowso.

"Miss Quick!" cried Legweak, waving his rope. "I got you this MATERIAL. It's synthetic fibre and Knuckles has a soup bone."

"Hmm, so I observe. Leave your stuff on the table by the door as you come in. And, Penny – do you really think it's right and proper to tell people that their heads are full of fungus?"

Penny Brown didn't have the nerve to say what she really thought, so she mumbled something that sounded like sorry.

In a very short time the table by the door was piled high with MATERIALS. Luckily, some of them were every bit as boring as a clay pot – that lump of chicken-wire, for example, beside the punctured rubber tyre. On the other hand, some were quite fascinating, like the gutta-percha gumshield used by boxers, and Jimmy Zest's glasscutter with its industrial diamonds. Zesty wanted to give a cutting demonstration, but Miss Quick said she was right out of glass. Instead, she asked Mandy Taylor to open her mystery box.

When the thing finally emerged, it had a handle, a long, thin body, and a round, flat end-piece. Only Legweak seemed to have a clue what it was.

"It's a Hoover!" he yelled.

"Miss Quick," said Mandy, "this is a metal detector, and if there's something made of metal under the ground, the machine will make a noise and you'll know it's there. Daddy says we could look for treasure."

110

At the mention of that word "treasure" eyes began to flash. Those boys looked like refugees from Long John Silver's gang.

"One never knows," laughed Miss Quick. "I once read about a farmer who found a golden necklace while ploughing his field, so these things do happen. Worth a fortune, it was. Now, let's classify our materials. We've already got plastic and clay and rubber and even diamonds to put on our chart."

Not to mention a cow bone, Penny Brown almost reminded her. What fun maths would be that morning if the caretaker's dog came looking for its property!

That evening Mandy Taylor and Penny Brown did their homework at Mandy's house. They had only just finished when Mandy's mother called up the stairs, saying, "Some friends of yours are at the front door, dear. Five boys. One of them seems to have a coal shovel."

The girls frowned at one another, for they were deeply suspicious. The five of them together? Why should Jimmy Zest and co suddenly pop up on Mandy's doorstep?

"Mandy? Please have some manners and come down and speak to your friends at once."

Now there was not a thing wrong with Mandy's manners – she was always polite and teachers said nice things about her on parents' evenings. But there are some people in the world upon whom good manners are totally wasted and, right now, five of them were packed into the new Edwardian glass porch at the front of her house.

Jimmy Zest clutched a roll of white paper, while Legweak – still wearing his rope – practically sat on a pot of geraniums. Gowso hovered gloomily at the back with a spade. He looked like a gravedigger. There was nothing gloomy about Nicholas Alexander, who was waving a filthy shovel in the air. A coal shovel.

"Well?" Mandy asked them.

"I like your greenhouse," said Legweak.

"It's not a greenhouse, it's a porch."

"Porch car," Shorty said, and nodded to himself mysteriously.

"Look, what do you all want?" Penny Brown asked. "We haven't much time because we have to go out."

Jimmy Zest unrolled a map of the old ruined castle up at Mercer's Wood.

"This is a photocopy, Amanda, I had it done in the town library this afternoon. Do you see the old castle grounds?"

"What about them?"

"There might be artefacts under the ground."

"He means *treasure*!" said Knuckles, with an eager twirl of the coal shovel.

The cunning schemers! Only now did the penny drop. They were after the metal detector. And they had come prepared with map, rope, spade and shovel.

"Maybe you'd lend us your metal Hoover for half an hour?" Legweak piped up cheerfully.

There was no "maybe" about it. Mandy Taylor knew that it would come back to her twisted up and useless, unable to detect metal ever again. The idea was unthinkable.

"It belongs to my uncle and my answer is No," she bravely told them, and quick as a flash took two steps backwards, closing the door as she went in case Nicholas Alexander should do something with the coal shovel. He had no understanding of the ordinary rules of life.

"Stick your metal detector up your jumper," said his voice beyond the closed door.

"And stick your shovel up yours," cried Penny Brown.

"It's not mine, it's Gowso's."

Typical. It wasn't even his own shovel. After a few more moans and groans, they opened the door and headed down the road, leaving Penny and Mandy with much to say about the sheer nerve of people who turned up at your front door and thought they had the right to borrow whatever they liked. Buried treasure, indeed!

All the same, they decided to be very careful the following day. It wasn't a good idea to take chances with the likes of Jimmy Zest, who could be crafty. As Mandy said, "Even as we speak he might be planning a horrible revenge."

By break-time next day, the girls knew that something shifty was going on. Jimmy Zest and co began to behave oddly – like a bunch of spies who have a big secret to hide.

During maths a note was passed from one to the other until it reached Legweak, who destroyed it by chewing. The mystery deepened during Art, when the boys all drew the same picture: zombies with outstretched arms and staring yellow eyes. Finally, Mandy Taylor overheard Jimmy Zest himself arranging to hold a secret meeting behind the bicycle shed. At lunch-time.

It was Penny's idea to tackle Legweak about all this. Legweak was one of those people who seemed to breathe different air from everybody else – a kind of laughing gas. Besides, he wasn't a quick thinker and could sometimes be outwitted.

"Right, Legweak, what's up?" she said to him.

"And don't say nothing because we've been watching you all morning," warned Mandy.

"A secret experiment," said Legweak.

"What kind of experiment?"

"I'm not telling you nothing," he said, jabbing a finger at Mandy. "If it wasn't for her we'd have found treasure and I'd have bought a horse."

And away he went, the poor treasureless thing.

"Right! We'll follow them," declared Penny Brown. "We'll wait behind the bicycle shed and soon see what they're up to. If they can be spies, so can we."

When lunch-time came they headed for the school's only bicycle shed along a guttery path that twisted in and out among prickly bushes and small trees. Mandy Taylor did a lot of complaining about dirty marks on her ankle socks and about drops of rain that dared to fall down the back of her neck.

"You'll not dissolve, Mandy," Penny whispered. "You're not a headache tablet."

"Suppose they find us spying on them?"

"Stop worrying. Shh! Here they come."

Before their very eyes something weird began to unfold. First of all Jimmy Zest took off his watch — the one that wouldn't leak even if you found yourself at the bottom of the Atlantic Ocean — and then set it swinging slowly to and fro in front of Legweak's eyes.

"Watch the watch," he kept saying. "Watch the watch. Watch the watch." And Legweak's head, watching the watch, moved like a spectator at a tennis match.

"He's hypnotizing him!" Mandy squeaked softly.

"Close your eyes," Jimmy Zest called out. "When you open them again, you will be my mind-slave until I click my fingers. Open your eyes."

The eyelids shot up, as if Legweak had just been switched on. Penny Brown could hardly believe her *own* eyes. Gone was the old Legweak, the happy, smiling face. In his place stood a robot, a blank-faced thing whose brain had slowly drained away.

"You are in the army," said Jimmy Zest.

Smart salute from Legweak. "There is a tank coming. It's getting closer. You will blow up the tank with your hand grenade."

Whereupon Legweak pulled the pin out of an imaginary grenade with his real teeth, and threw it. Shorty actually ducked. Mandy Taylor muttered that this sort of thing should not be allowed.

There was more. "You are wearing a suit of armour," shouted Jimmy Zest, and Legweak staggered forward on stiff legs. You could almost hear him clanking. Then Zesty clicked his fingers and Legweak looked around him, beaming – his old self once again. He didn't seem to have the foggiest memory of blasting a tank.

The girls scampered away.

"That isn't right," Mandy Taylor said indignantly. "He's got no business turning people into mind-slaves. Mucking about with someone else's brain is serious, you know."

Penny Brown couldn't agree more. Imagine turning your friend into a walking zombie! This was yet more proof that you had to watch Jimmy Zest like a hawk.

The next day, as it happened, two people from Miss Quick's class were on litter duty in the playground: Nicholas Alexander and Jimmy Zest. But they didn't do their litter duty. Their mind-slave did it for them.

Mandy Taylor and Penny Brown watched their grisly plan in operation. A crisp bag flew by. Legweak went after it like a clockwork toy that's

just been wound up. Behind him came Knuckles with his lazy hands in his pockets and a smirk on his face – and, of course, Jimmy Zest, the controlling master. Legweak pounced on the crisp bag and popped it into a bin.

"They've done it again," cried Mandy. "They're making him do their litter duty, would you believe."

The girls marched boldly across the playground. "Legweak! Jimmy Zest has taken you over. Your mind is not your own!"

No answer came. His eyes looked through them, seeing something in the far beyond. Legweak wasn't a true person any more, he was a puppet. Miss Quick must be found and told about this if Legweak was to be rescued from the clutches of Jimmy Zest.

But Miss Quick was in the staff-room, and the girls hesitated when they came to the staff-room door. There were sixteen teachers in there, all eating sandwiches and probably discussing the world's political problems.

"Maybe we should wait?" Mandy whispered.

"Mandy, any teacher would want to know about a case of mind-slavery. One brain isn't enough for Jimmy Zest, he wants Legweak's as well! And why not a hundred minds? Our school could be full of hypnotized zombies by home time."

Penny Brown tapped on the door and Miss Watson poked her head out.

"Excuse me, please, I wonder could we speak urgently to Miss Quick?"

Miss Quick arrived, rustling a newspaper, frowning slightly. "Won't this wait until after lunch, girls?"

"Miss Quick, we think Jimmy Zest is in control of someone else's *mind*."

The teacher's eyelids flickered, then stayed open rather wide. After a pause she blinked once more, and said, "Er . . . whose mind, exactly?"

"Legweak's," said Penny. "Stephen Armstrong, Miss. Jimmy Zest makes him watch the watch and turns him into a mind-slave until he clicks his fingers. He is being . . ."

"Manipulated," said Mandy, whose vocabulary was excellent.

Miss Quick said "Hmm" as if she liked the sound of *manipulated*. She loved big words. "How is this happening, exactly?"

"Hypnotism!" said Penny Brown. "Zesty steers him round the playground like a robot picking up litter. He makes him watch the watch and turns him into a mind-slave until he clicks his fingers. Yesterday he made him join the army and fight tanks."

A kind of drumming noise began, made by Miss Quick's fingers on the staff-room door. "You don't think it's some kind of game?"

"Miss Quick, we have seen this happen," cried Mandy.

"I see. Hmm. Hypnotism and mind-slavery. Well, leave it with me and I'll look into it after lunch. Sort things out. OK?"

As good as her word, Miss Quick wrote HYPNOTISM in big letters across the board when class began that afternoon. *Flute*, thought Penny Brown, *she's not wasting any time*. She glanced over at Jimmy Zest and he actually had the cheek to smile at her.

Hypnotism, Miss Quick explained, was a

sleeplike condition sometimes used by doctors to help certain kinds of patients. A person who had been hypnotized often did things that he couldn't remember afterwards, and often behaved as if he were under the control of the hypnotizer.

And that was as far as she got. Up rose Shorty in a state of excitement. "Miss, Zesty can do that! He wiggles his watch and Legweak conks out. Show her, Legweak!"

Off came the watch. The smile on Legweak's face would have made a crocodile jealous – until he watched the watch. Now he looked as blank as a plastic dummy in a shop window.

"There is something burning," said Jimmy Zest spookily. "You definitely smell something burning, Legweak."

One sniff, two sniffs. Legweak peered around, nose twitching like a rabbit's.

"You have to find what's burning, Legweak!"

All of a sudden, Legweak took off on a tour of the classroom, following his nose. After some wild sniffing he pounced on Mandy Taylor's schoolbag. Penny Brown noticed that Gowso was in fits. Did that sprouting big mushroom know something? "Send for the fire brigade!" shouted Legweak. "There's a fire in this bag. Help! Nine-nine-nine."

Naturally, Mandy Taylor stood up with a face like thunder and snatched her bag back. A hint of a smile had appeared on Miss Quick's face.

"And how do you get him out of this hypnotic trance?" she asked Jimmy Zest.

"Dead easy," said Legweak himself. "He clicks his fingers like this and I just snap out of it." And so saying, Legweak clicked his own fingers.

At that moment, Penny Brown *knew*. Legweak could not have clicked his own fingers. Not if he'd been hypnotized.

"It was only a game, Miss Quick," said Jimmy Zest.

Legweak had never been hypnotized. Penny Brown and Mandy Taylor sat there knowing that Jimmy Zest had dreamed up the whole mind-slave scheme just to fool then into a snare.

The fun, Miss Quick decided, was now over. She said the time had come for Silent Reading and that Stephen Armstrong would most likely win a Hollywood Oscar one day.

The two girls had a hard time going home that afternoon. It's not easy walking down the road in front of goonies shouting, "WE ARE THE ZOMBIE MIND-SLAVES, HA, HA, HA."

"Ignore them, Mandy," advised Penny Brown. "Never speak to them again. I feel humiliated.

And *she* had no business smiling, you know."

"Who?"

"Our teacher. An Oscar, indeed! Some people are easily impressed."

"She did say that it might be only a game, Penny."

"Game my foot! And some people need taking down a peg or two. Some people had better watch out."

She was referring, of course, to the bunch of zombie mind-slaves hooting along behind. *Just you wait, Jimmy Zest*, she was thinking. There would be revenge and it would be sweet. Those boys were going to feel so small they'd think they were *invisible*.

Soon it would be her turn to smile.

Miss Quick's class was in the Hall.

It was their job, that afternoon, to set out chairs for a big meeting in the school that night. Jimmy Zest appointed himself boss of the chair-shifters, and while he got on with it, Mandy Taylor and Penny Brown cornered Gowso.

"Gowso, lend us your spade this afternoon, would you? We're taking the metal detector up to the old castle and we need something to dig up treasure with. You could come too if you like."

"Me?"

"And your spade."

"Me and my spade?" Gowso seemed over-whelmed. "Yeah, OK."

Off he zoomed to spread the news. Sure enough, inside thirty seconds Legweak appeared, along with Jimmy Zest, and his faithful Rottweiler, Nicholas Alexander.

"Is it true you're going treasure hunting with your metal Hoover?" asked Legweak.

"Yes, it is true," said Mandy. "Why?"

"Need a rope? I could bring my special synthetic fibre rope."

"Well, we *are* hoping to find brooches and rings and things," said Penny Brown. "And ancient armour, of course. And gold coins with the heads of emperors and Vikings. There must be millions of things just waiting for people to dig them up again and a rope might be useful. You can come if you like, Legweak."

"Yes!" Legweak punched the air.

"What about my map?" asked Jimmy Zest.

"I'm coming too," said Knuckles.

"Have you never heard the word 'please'?" Mandy asked him bravely. "Isn't it in your dictionary?"

"Me and Shorty haven't got a dictionary."

"I've got one that talks," said Gowso.

Mandy gave a sigh. "Look, forget I spoke, OK? You can *all* come, so long as there's no messing about with my uncle's metal detector. Be outside my house at four o'clock exactly."

There had been no "please". Would there now be a "thank you"? Not at all. Away they went, squabbling already over who was having Gowso's spade, and who would have to make do with the coal shovel.

By a quarter past four, then, the band of treasure-hunters was on its way. In Penny Brown's opinion there wasn't a lot to see up at the castle. Some fragments of ancient walls stuck up like broken teeth, that was all. Then Jimmy Zest pointed to a place that might have been a gate, and began to talk about important lords and ladies passing to and fro, all dripping with the finest of jewellery. There might even be golden candlesticks.

"I'm buying a horse for my synthetic fibre rope," Legweak announced, thinking of his share of the loot.

After twenty minutes or so they had dug up the springs of a mattress, the skeleton of a pram, and a crushed bicycle wheel; no sign yet of anything precious. Continuing clockwise round the walls they came upon a large hollow with a circle of blackened stones at its centre. There had been a fire here at one time.

"Barbecue," Penny guessed.

"Or witches," said Gowso. "They sometimes take all their clothes off and dance about at midnight."

Six faces turned as one to stare at Gowso, wondering how he came to know such a thing. *Maybe that talking dictionary*, thought Legweak.

Suddenly the metal detector found its voice again and began to whine.

"Got something," cried Mandy.

"Spade," called Zesty.

Knuckles drove in the spade, striking metal. "I saw something down there. It looked like gold."

This was enough to quicken the heartbeat of any human being. Gold! The one metal that drives people wild. Jimmy Zest, waving away the crude spade, now used his fingers to flick away the fine soil still covering most of the object.

With thumping hearts and goggle-eyes they stared at what seemed to be an ancient, golden shield. Until Mandy said, "Wow!" very quietly you could have heard a cuckoo call on the planet Mars.

"But what is it?" whispered Gowso.

"It must be ornamental armour," said Zesty.

"Gold doesn't rust, you see, this might have belonged to the King himself. It's worth . . . a *fortune*."

Knuckles picked up the shield. Through the clinging soil you could see the gleam of dull gold. Breathless with emotion, he spoke. "We split this seven ways, right?"

"You mean with a hacksaw?" asked Shorty.

"For heaven's sakes, *Shorty*," said Mandy Taylor, "he means sell it and split the money, not saw the thing into bits. And don't rub at it, Knuckles, my mum knows about antiques and you're not supposed to clean them."

There was some crazy talk about money and the price of gold and whether the Queen might own this shield and how she wasn't getting it back even if she did; but the main problem was how to get this wonderful thing home. They walked slowly down the road in a sort of moving circle to protect it from the eyes of the public. Gowso, out in front, carried his spade aloft, as if he was proud of it.

At Mandy's gate they had a short talk about where to keep the shield until it could be brought into school next day for Miss Quick to admire.

"I'll keep it in my house," said Mandy.

"Why?" Knuckles asked suspiciously.

"Has your house got a burglar alarm?" Penny Brown asked him. "No it hasn't, so that's why. Could the police be at your house in two minutes flat if burglars broke in? No. So goodbye."

The girls marched up Mandy's path. Inside her garage they set the shield up on a bench beside a heavy hammer and a can of golden paint-spray.

They didn't even try to keep the smiles off their faces.

Penny Brown had hardly finished her boiled egg in the morning when she got an urgent phone call.

"Penny, hurry up and get over here, they're outside and staring in at me already, all of them. Legweak is lassoing our stone lions with his stupid rope and my mother wants to know what they're *doing* out there."

Penny got round to Mandy's in less than five minutes, going in by the back door. None of those boys would take a step away from her gate until the golden shield had been seen, so the girls let them have a quick peek into the plastic bag.

"I won't unwrap it," said Mandy, "in case it gets damaged between here and school."

Jimmy Zest and Knuckles, who insisted on carrying the shield, led the way down the road, followed by a miserable-looking Gowso, then came Legweak wearing his blue rope, and finally Penny Brown and Mandy Taylor.

"Legweak," said Penny, "why are you bringing that rope to school yet again?"

"It's made of synthetic fibre."

"We know that! If I hear you saying synthetic fibre one more time I think I'll be sick."

"Synthetic fibre," said Legweak.

Whereupon Penny Brown stormed ahead, not to be sick, but to escape from one of the world's outstanding idiots.

Then Gowso began to complain. "We've got no coal shovel, you know. It's up at that castle somewhere and I got shouted at. My mum says I lose everything."

"You could easily convert to gas or electric," Mandy advised, "it's much, much cleaner."

"Never worry your head, Gowso," shouted Shorty. "You'll soon be able to buy ten million coal shovels."

"Or a horse!" whooped Legweak.

They were all in fine form by the time they reached school that morning. Unfortunately, Miss Quick happened to be late. She rushed in and opened up her roll-book like someone in a hurry to call out names in world-record time.

Knuckles could bear the suspense no longer.

Up he surged, holding the golden shield aloft. "Miss Quick, look what I've got, pure gold from history and there's maybe more. Zesty says it belonged to the King."

"Of England!" cried Shorty.

Unbelievable pandemonium broke out. Mandy Taylor glanced uneasily in the direction of Penny Brown as Nicholas Alexander set off on a tour of the classroom. It was awesome. The place looked like a football final – except that football fans don't normally wave synthetic-fibre ropes above their heads. Miss Quick calmly removed the golden trophy from Knuckles's sticky fingers, and returned to examine it at her desk.

"Could I make a guess about this?" she said. "Did you use Amanda's metal detector, by any chance?"

"And Gowso's spade, Miss," shouted Shorty, to be fair.

Miss Quick silenced him with a stare before switching her attention to Mandy and Penny. "And were *you* there, girls, when this wonderful golden shield was miraculously discovered?"

Penny mumbled something that sounded like "yes". It was obvious by now that Miss Quick had put two and two together. She was a teacher, after all, she could add up.

"I see. How lucky can you get? Tell me, Jimmy

Zest, which King of England owned it, do you think?"

That was the moment when Jimmy Zest glanced sideways and looked Penny Brown straight in the eye. She looked away, pretending to hunt for something deep down in her pencil case.

"Well . . . we haven't had a chance to examine it yet," said Jimmy Zest. "Not properly. It might not be the real thing."

"It's the real thing, all right," said Miss Quick. "Once a bin-lid always a bin-lid, even if it *has* been bashed flat with a hammer and painted gold. Wouldn't you say so, Penny?"

The head of Penny Brown began to nod as if butter wouldn't melt in its innocent little mouth. This was her way of avoiding trouble.

"Now look, you people – let's call this a one-all draw, shall we? I want no more hypnotized zombies prancing about the playground and no more golden oldies that once belonged to the King of England. Or it's trouble! Understood?"

Perfect peace returned to the classroom as they prepared for spellings. Legweak folded his rope, a wonderful smile upon his face even though he still had no treasure and no horse. Shorty winked at Penny Brown as he sharpened one of Gowso's pencils away to almost nothing. The frown had returned to Gowso's face as he worried about his disappearing pencil, or his lost coal shovel, or perhaps the coming spellings. Then Mandy poked Penny joyfully in the ribs, and there was Jimmy Zest giving them a tail-between-the-legs sort of grin. Penny Brown thought that if there are moments of pure gold, this was one of them.

But when they looked over at Nicholas Alexander, there was murder in those terrible eyes. Best to keep out of that baboon's way for a day or two, they reckoned.

Sam McBratney

ZESTY

Jimmy Zest is never short of *good* ideas. At least, *he* thinks they're good. But his friends don't always agree, as they're the ones who seem to get the blame when things go *wrong*.

Still, why worry about that when there's fowl play in the park to be uncovered, horse-hair tails to be discovered and a missing tortoise to be recovered?

The second collection of cracking Jimmy Zest stories.

'Delightfully comic . . . sympathetic and credible' *Guardian*

A selected list of titles available from Macmillan Children's Books

The prices shown below are correct at the time of going to press. However, Macmillan Publishers reserve the right to show new retail prices on covers which may differ from those previously advertised.

SAM McBRATNEY

Jimmy Zest	0 330 39986 1	£3.99
Zesty	0 330 39987 X	£3.99
Jimmy Zest, Super Pest	0 330 40047 9	£3.99
Jimmy Zest is Best!	0 330 40048 7	£3.99

All Macmillan titles can be ordered at your local bookshop or are available by post from:

Book Service by Post
PO Box 29, Douglas, Isle of Man IM99 1BQ

Credit cards accepted. For details:
Telephone: 01624 675137
Fax: 01624 670923
E-mail: bookshop@enterprise.net

Free postage and packing in the UK.
Overseas customers: add £1 per book (paperback)
and £3 per book (hardback).